Yo, Vikings!

Book and Lyrics by
Marcus Stevens

Music by
Sam Willmott

A SAMUEL FRENCH ACTING EDITION

SAMUEL FRENCH

FOUNDED 1830

SAMUELFRENCH.COM
SAMUELFRENCH-LONDON.CO.UK

MUSIC USE NOTE

Licensees are solely responsible for obtaining formal written permission from copyright owners to use copyrighted music in the performance of this play and are strongly cautioned to do so. If no such permission is obtained by the licensee, then the licensee must use only original music that the licensee owns and controls. Licensees are solely responsible and liable for all music clearances and shall indemnify the copyright owners of the play(s) and their licensing agent, Samuel French, against any costs, expenses, losses and liabilities arising from the use of music by licensees. Please contact the appropriate music licensing authority in your territory for the rights to any incidental music.

RENTAL MATERIALS

An orchestration consisting of a **Piano/Vocal Score**, along with **Rehearsal and Performance Tracks**, will be loaned two months prior to the production ONLY on the receipt of the Licensing Fee quoted for all performances, the rental fee and a refundable deposit. Please contact Samuel French for perusal of the music materials as well as a performance license application.

IMPORTANT BILLING AND CREDIT REQUIREMENTS

If you have obtained performance rights to this title, please refer to your licensing agreement for important billing and credit requirements.

YO, VIKINGS! received its world premiere at Upper Darby Summer Stage (Harry Dietzler, Producer) in Upper Darby, Pennsylvania on July 21, 2010. The performance was directed by Marcus Stevens, assistant directed by Rachel Stevens, and music directed by Eric Thompson. The sets were designed by Lindsay Mayer, with lights by Chuck Reese. The cast was as follows:

EMMA KATZ	Rachel Costello
JUDY KATZ	Rachel Medori
DAD	Clay McDermott
SIGURD TORVALDSSON	Sean Skahill
OLLIE KATZ	Tim Braithwaite
MRS. MUKHERJEE	Tyleah Hawkins
BOTHVAR/MOVING MAN	Tristan Horan
NIKKI TIBBLES	Emily Butz
ZINZI FERDINAND-MUÑOZ	Barb Kurmlavage
SEBBY FERDINAND-MUÑOZ	Jonathan McNamee
MURPHY BEAN	Bobby Loftus
GUNNHILD	Trez Malatesta
OLAF	Matt Lantieri
HELGA	Bonnie Baldini
THORKLE	Jared Gross

CLASSMATES/VIKINGS . . . . Brian Mann, Maddy Pelesh, Michelle McElwee, Adam Schwartz, Mara Baratka, Taylor Barett, Katie Lynch, Emily Lunardi, Lachlan Blubaugh, Amanda Bradley, Sharon Brown, Rachel Coler, Rebecca Costello, Bridget Hegarty, Katie Jordan, Allie Knorr, Bianca LoGiurato, Matt Magargee, Diana Manners, Michelle Bartkus, Katie Barton, Katie Lynch, Jason Boyer, Colleen Mann, Rachel Brodie, Kate McDermott, Kara McGee, Courtney Brown, Julie Cahill, Catherine McGurk, Laura Cahill, Ellyn McGurk, Olivia Cicalese, Connor McGlaughlin, Krista Delone, Anna Melone, Etta DiMarco, Valerie Mertin, Becky Dooling, Kelly Milligan, Sue Dougherty, Joe Paparo, Mason Fisher, Kyle Murray, Emily Glackin, Sam Murray, Anthony Paparo, Karen Shantz, Melanie Siracusa, Lauryn Thomas, Emily Todd, Katherine Woods, Rob Katz, Marcy Sutter, Arden Vizzard, Anna Landau-Smith, Christie Lodge, Jimmy Wyatt,

YO, VIKINGS! received its West Coast premiere at Children's Musical Theaterworks (Judy Stene, Executive Director) in Fresno, California on March 2, 2012. The performance was directed by Skyler Gray, with sets by Ian Loveall, costumes by Trina Short, lighting by Laura Vogt, and sound by Charles Ottavio. The cast was as follows:

EMMA KATZ . . . . .Catriona Fray and Genevieve Becker (alternating)

JUDY KATZ/MJÖLVERK. . . . . Shannah Estep

SIGURD TORVALDSSON . . . . George Akina

OLLIE KATZ . . . . Luke Teixeira

MRS. MUKHERJEE . . . . .Kylie Briggs

BOTHVAR/MOVING MAN. . . . . Greg Ruud

NIKKI TIBBLES/GUNNHILD. . . . . Kyla Kennedy

ZINZI FERDINAND-MUÑOZ/HELGA . . . . .Hannah Moser

SEBBY FERDINAND-MUÑOZ/OLAF . . . . Bryce Moser

MURPHY BEAN/THORKLE. . . . . Daniel Hernandez

CLASSMATES/VIKINGS . . . . .Jackie King, David Marinovich,
Jacob Williams, Catriona Fray, Genevieve Becker

CHARACTERS

EMMA KATZ – Fox, monkfish, fifth grader, Viking

MOM (JUDY KATZ) – Emma's mom
Also plays **MJÖLVERK** – a frost giant

SIGURD TORVALDSSON – Librarian, dragon slayer

OLLIE KATZ – Emma's brother, a kindergartner
(can be played by a young girl)

MRS. MUKHERJEE – Emma's teacher

BOTHVAR, THE FORK-SPLITTER – a Viking
Also plays **MOVING MAN** – a moving man

NIKKI TIBBLES – Emma's classmate
Also plays **GUNNHILD, THE SHE-BEAR** – a Viking

ZINZI FERDINAND-MUÑOZ – Emma's classmate
Also plays **HELGA, THE CLANG-FIST** – a Viking

SEBBY FERDINAND-MUÑOZ – Emma's classmate
Also plays **OLAF, THE BOORISH** – a Viking

MURPHY BEAN – Emma's classmate
Also plays **THORKLE, THE TRAVELER** – a Viking

PASHA
PHYLLIS
GUNTHER } Emma's Classmates, also Vikings
SIMON

Plus any additional Vikings, Townspeople, and Kids (*if desired*)

SETTING

Swarthmore, PA: The Present
Iceland and Beyond: 985 A.D.

SCENE BREAKDOWN AND MUSICAL NUMBERS

PROLOGUE – SWARTHMORE, P.A. AND ENVIRONS

"You Gotta Believe" . . . . **EMMA & COMPANY**

"You Gotta Believe Play-Off" . . . . *Instrumental*

SCENE 1 – INT. MRS. MUKHERJEE'S CLASSROOM

"The Rules/World Discovery Day" . . . .**MRS. MUKHERJEE & EMMA**

"World Discovery Day Play-Off" . . . . *Instrumental*

SCENE 2 – A SCHOOL HALLWAY / INT. EMMA'S HOUSE

SCENE 3 – INT. LIBRARY

"The Library" . . . . *Instrumental*

"Into the Storm". . . . . **MR. SIGURD, BOTHVAR, & VIKINGS**

"Emma the Red" . . . .**EMMA & VIKINGS**

"Emma the Red Play-Off" . . . . *Instrumental*

SCENE 4 – INT. EMMA'S HOUSE

SCENE 5 – INT. MRS. MUKHERJEE'S CLASSROOM

"Emma Goes to School" . . . . *Instrumental*

"Keep on Sailing" . . . . **MR. SIGURD, MRS. MUKHERJEE & KIDS**

"Keep on Sailing (Reprise)" . . . . **MR. SIGURD**

SCENE 6 – EXT. SCHOOLYARD / JOTUNHEIM

"Emma the Red (Reprise)" . . . . **OLLIE, EMMA**

"The Prayer" . . . . **BOTHVAR & VIKINGS**

"The Asgard Vessel" . . . . *Instrumental*

SCENE 7 – INT. EMMA'S HOUSE

"I Love You, But No" . . . . **MOM**

"The Letter" . . . . **EMMA**

SCENE 8 – EXT. PLAYGROUND

"Sally Intro One" . . . . *Instrumental*

"Sally Intro Two" . . . . *Instrumental*

"The Terrible Tale of Sally Shapiro" . . . . .**NIKKI, ZINZI, SEBBY, MURPHY**

"Sally Play-Off" . . . . *Instrumental*

SCENE 9 – EXT. LIBRARY / INT. LIBRARY

"World Discovery Day (Reprise)" . . . .**MRS. MUKHERJEE & KIDS**

"The Dragon Slayer" . . . . *Instrumental*

SCENE 10 – EXT. A CURB OUTSIDE THE LIBRARY

"Emma the Red (Reprise 2)" . . . . **EMMA**

"Real Adventure" . . . . **MOM**

"Real Adventure Play-Off" . . . . *Instrumental*

SCENE 11 – INT. MRS. MUKHERJEE'S CLASSROOM
SCENE 12 – EXT. EMMA'S BACKYARD / EXT. LIBRARY

"The Birthday Party" . . . . *Instrumental*
"Yo, Vikings!" . . . . **COMPANY**
"Bows and Exit Music" . . . . *Instrumental*

For Harry Dietzler and Upper Darby Summer Stage
– Marcus

For Jean Boatman Jamgochian
– Sam

PROLOGUE

(Lightning and thunder. Shadows flutter across the stage: flashes of dragons and ships. Figures with helmets and shields lurk in the darkness.)

MUSIC NO. 1:
"YOU GOTTA BELIEVE"

VIKINGS.

OH, OH, OH, AH, OH, AH, AH, AH, AH, AH!

*(Light rise on **EMMA**, her eyes fixed on something. We hear **MOM** in the distance, her voice distorted.)*

EMMA.

I HAVE WAITED, I HAVE WONDERED

MOM. Emma?

EMMA.

WHEN WILL ADVENTURE FIND ME?

MOM. Emma…

EMMA.

WHAT CAN I DO TO MAKE EVERYONE SEE ME?

MOM. Emma!

EMMA.

HOW WILL I KNOW WHO I SHOULD –

*(**MOM**'s voice suddenly rings clearly and directly, snapping **EMMA** out of her fantasy.)*

MOM. Emma Katz! Get down here this instant!

EMMA. *(Racing off)* Coming!

*(Lights rise on EXT. SWARTHMORE, PA. **MOM** enters holding **EMMA**'s lunch, followed by **OLLIE**.)*

MOM. You're going to be late for school again! Uch, that girl…

OLLIE. *(With a speech impediment)* Emma! Huwwie up!

MOM. Emma...!?

EMMA. *(Off)* Coming! Wait'll you see!

MOM.

> WHAT'S YOUR PLAN, EMMA?
> PLEASE, ON MY KNEES
> MUST YOU ALWAYS KEEP US ON OUR TOES?
> IF YOU CAN, EMMA,
> DO GIVE A CLUE
> 'CUZ WHAT EMMA'S THINKIN', NO ONE KNOWS!
> WHAT'S IN YOUR BRAIN
> WE CAN NEVER EXPLAIN
> AND WE'LL NEVER BE SURE
> 'TIL WE SEE WHO YOU'LL BE
> AS YOU SHOUT, COMING OUT THAT DOOR!
>
> *(**EMMA** enters as a "FOX," wearing furry ears on her head and a bushy, red tail.)*

EMMA.

> AND I'M A FOX, I'M A FOX!
> I'M A SCRUFFY, FLUFFY FOX
> I'M NO GIRL, I HUNT SQUIRREL
> THEY'RE MY PREY!
> I'M A BEAST, NOT A CHILD
> 'CUZ I'D RATHER ROAM THE WILD
> AND YOU GOTTA BELIEVE
> THAT I'M WHO I SAY!

MOM. No, Emma. You can't wear that to school.

EMMA. Why not? This is my true calling, Mom! Foxes are awesome. We scavenge and we travel in packs. Everyone in Swarthmore's gonna want to join my pack. Promise.

MOM. I'm pretty sure foxes travel alone, Emma. And *you* certainly will if you go to school like that.

EMMA. But –

MOM. But nothing. I can't have you mauling someone again.

EMMA. I told you. I was a Velociraptor and I was seriously provoked.

(**MOM** *points towards the door sternly.* **EMMA** *removes her ears and trudges back inside the house.* **OLLIE** *follows her. The scene shifts to…INT. MRS. MUKHERJEE'S CLASSROOM.* **MRS. MUKHERJEE** *enters.*)

MOM. I'm so sorry I'm late, Mrs. Mukherjee. How's she doing in class? Is she in trouble?

MRS. MUKHERJEE. Mrs. Katz, I'm actually afraid to teach a new lesson for fear that Emma will morph into something I can't handle. Last week she was Ben Franklin, and yesterday she was a plant cell…

EMMA'S SMART
EVEN SO, YOU SHOULD KNOW
HER BEHAVIOR'S GOTTA CHANGE, AND HOW!
FOR A START
I CONFESS THAT HER DRESS
IS DISTRACTING, WHICH I CAN'T ALLOW
SHE GETS KINDA CRAZED
AND THE CLASS'LL GET DAZED
WHICH IS PROB'LY HER GOAL
SHE MISLEADS AND PROCEEDS
TO CONFUSE, SO I LOSE ALL CONTROL!

(**EMMA** *enters in a "MONKFISH" costume – something she clearly made herself. She is followed by OLLIE, dressed as a "SQUID."*)

EMMA.
NOW I'M A MONKFISH, I'M A MONKFISH!
I'M A SWISHY, SQUISHY MONKFISH!
I'VE GOT SCALES, I'VE MET WHALES
AND A SQUID!
I'D GROW GILLS, DON'T YOU SEE,
TO BE ANYTHING BUT ME
SO YOU GOTTA BELIEVE
THAT I'M NOT A KID!

MOM. Emma, take that off. Now. You have to stop doing this.

MRS. MUKHERJEE. *(Simultaneous with* **MOM***)* Emma, this is not appropriate behavior for a fifth grader.

*(***EMMA** *runs out of the classroom.)*

EMMA.
I DO IT 'CUZ IT MAKES EACH DAY EXCITING
AND I DON'T NEED A REASON OR A RHYME
THE STORY KEEPS ON CHANGING AS I'M WRITING
ALL THE TIME
IT CAN CHANGE ON A DIME!

*(***EMMA** *sheds her "MONKFISH" to reveal a "DENTIST" costume.)*

NOW I'M A DENTIST, I'M A DENTIST!
I'M A HIGHLY QUALIFIED DENTIST
I'VE GOT SKILL WITH MY DRILL
AND MY TOOLS

MRS. MUKHERJEE & MOM.
EMMA, PLEASE! THIS WON'T DO
WE JUST WANT YOU TO BE YOU

EMMA.
THEN YOU GOTTA BELIEVE
THAT I MAKE MY OWN RULES

*(***EMMA** *runs off.* **OLLIE** *follows her.* **MUKHERJEE** *and* **MOM** *exit. A bell rings and the* **KIDS** *enter.)*

NIKKI. She's so weird. Every time she reads something or sees something or anything, she changes.

MURPHY. Yesterday she told me she was Robin Hood. She gave me two quarters and a stick of butter.

ZINZI. She told me she was a Shaman, and that I was healed.

SEBBY. My rabbit's been afraid of chairs ever since that "Lion Tamer Incident."

NIKKI.
EMMA'S NUTS

SEBBY.
EMMA'S DENSE

MURPHY.
SHE'S INTENSE

ZINZI.

WELL, SHE MARCHES TO A DIFFERENT TUNE

NIKKI.

SHE'S A KLUTZ

MURPHY.

SHE'S UNCOOL

NIKKI.

SHE'S A FOOL

SEBBY & ZINZI.

AND HER MIND IS ALWAYS ON THE MOON!

KIDS.

AND EV'RY DAY
NO ONE EVER CAN SAY
WHAT THE GIRL'S GONNA DO
'CUZ HER DREAMS
ARE EXTREMES
AND THERE'S ALWAYS SOMETHING NEW!

(**EMMA** *enters as a "SQUASH." The entire town trickles in to witness her antics.*)

EMMA.	**KIDS.**
AND I'M A SQUASH, I'M A SQUASH I'M A YELLOW, MELLOW SQUASH AS A GOURD, I AIN'T BORED I GOT SEEDS! WHAT SEEMS LAME –	
	Lame!
– CAN BE FUN	
	Yeah right!
OR IT WILL BE WHEN I'M DONE	
	Aah – why aren't you done?
AND YOU GOTTA BELIEVE IT'S WHAT EVERYBODY NEEDS!	

ALL.

> THE KID IS CLEARLY HEARING HER OWN DRUMMER
> IT HAS TO BE A PHASE SHE'LL JUST OUTGROW
> YOU SHOULD HAVE SEEN HER PIRATE QUEEN LAST SUMMER
> GOES TO SHOW
> WITH THAT GIRL, WHO CAN KNOW?

> *(Throughout the next passage,* **EMMA** *appears here, there, and everywhere in a wild array of eclectic get-ups.)*

ALL.

> SHE GOES TO THE DOCTOR
> AND THEN SHE'S A SURGEON
> SHE READS ABOUT OCEANS
> AND THEN SHE'S A STURGEON

> SHE PLAYS IN THE KITCHEN
> AND THEN SHE'S A BLENDER
> SHE GOES TO THE BANK
> AND SHE GOES LEGAL TENDER

> SHE'S OUT AT THE AIRPORT
> AND THAT GIRL IS FLYIN'
> SHE LEARNS HOW TO HULA
> AND THEN SHE'S HAWAIIAN
> SHE GOES TO THE ZOO
> AND IN TWO SHE'S A LIONESS
> OH, YES!

> AT HER SCHOOL, IN A SHOP
> WITH A COSTUME AND A PROP
> AND SHE'LL NEVER BE THE SAME
> AND SHE'LL SWEAR IT'S NOT A GAME
> AND WITH A PAPER CROWN
> SHE'LL TAKE THIS TOWN
> AND TURN IT UPSIDE DOWN!

> *(***EMMA** *enters as an* "AMOEBA.")

EMMA.

> AND I'M AN AMOEBA, I'M AN AMOEBA!
> I'M AN AMOEBA-MEBA-MEBA-MEBA-MEBA-

MOM. Emma! Go inside and put on something appropriate for school. NOW.

(The world around **EMMA** *freezes.)*

EMMA.

BUT IT'S TRUE
WHY CAN'T YOU UNDERSTAND?
I'M ALONE IN MY SCHEMES
WON'T YOU JOIN ME IN MY DREAMS?

*(***EMMA*** sneakily reaches into her backpack, revealing her fox ears and tail. She puts them on gleefully.)*

EMMA.

MORE ADVENTURES STILL AWAIT
AND I PROMISE THEY'LL BE GREAT
AND THEY'RE UP MY SLEEVE
IF YOU WOULD JUST BELIEVE!

(The world springs back to life.)

ALL.

SHE'S A MONK! SHE'S A SKUNK!
SHE'S A WORM! SHE'S A GERM!
SHE'S A BOAT! SHE'S A GOAT!
SHE'S A BOAR! SHE'S A SPORE!
SHE'S A COOK! SHE'S A CROOK!
SHE'S A FLY! SHE'S A SPY!
SHE'S THE POPE! SHE'S A POX!

EMMA.

I'M A FOX!

(Everyone looks at her, perplexed and exasperated.)

MUSIC NO. 2:
"YOU GOTTA BELIEVE PLAY-OFF"

(A bell rings and the scene segues to…)

SCENE ONE –
INT. MRS. MUKHERJEE'S CLASSROOM

(**MRS. MUKHERJEE** *stands at the blackboard.*)

MRS. MUKHERJEE. Friends. Settle down, please. And please move your seats into our reading formation. Thank you, sir. Thank you, lady…
(*To* **EMMA:**)
Thank you…rodent. Plenty to do, plenty to do…
(*She busies herself.*)

MURPHY. Hey, Emma! You look weirder than you did yesterday. What are you? A beaver?

EMMA. I'm a fox!

SEBBY. Emma, dress-up is kind of a second grade thing.

ZINZI. Well said, Brother.

SEBBY. Personally, I find this behavior to be off-putting.

PHYLLIS. The Ferdinand-Muñoz twins do have a point, Emma.

EMMA. It's not dress up! People, a fox is the coolest thing you could ever be. You guys will love it. We can all be in the same pack, and I'll get my wagon and give fox rides to the park. Hey, Nikki, don't you want an adventure like that?

NIKKI. (*Dripping with sarcasm*) Oh sure, Emma. I mean who wouldn't?

ZINZI. I do kind of like the tail.

NIKKI. Zinzi! Shh!

(*Makes a "Zip it" gesture.*)

ZINZI. OK.

EMMA. I mean it, you guys! Wait'll you see how awesome it is to be a nocturnal predator, stalking your unsuspecting prey!

(*She stands on a chair and growls.*)

MRS. MUKHERJEE. Emma! Emma, get down right now.

EMMA. But I was showing Nikki Tibbles that –

MRS. MUKHERJEE. Doesn't matter. This is a classroom. We're not here to play at being a racoon.

EMMA. I'm a fox!

MRS. MUKHERJEE. Fox, racoon, gerbil, hamster! When will it stop?

EMMA. When I find my calling, Mrs. Mukherjee. When I find what I'm truly supposed to be, I'll stop. Promise.

MRS. MUKHERJEE. And what are we supposed to do until then? Emma, I just want you to be a part of the class. That's all. Whatever you are, I'd like you to be a part of things. Not on the outside, stirring up trouble.

EMMA. *(Sitting)* Maybe everyone else is on the outside.

MRS. MUKHERJEE. Well, now that we're all settled… Friends, I would like to talk about your next research presentation.

MURPHY. Aww, Mrs. Mukherjee. Do we have to?

MRS. MUKHERJEE. I'm afraid we have to, Murphy Bean.

MUSIC NO. 3:
"THE RULES/WORLD DISCOVERY DAY"

(She flips the blackboard over to show the words "WORLD DISCOVERY DAY.")

PASHA. World Discovery Day?

MRS. MUKHERJEE. "Celebrating Exploration and the Spirit of Adventure."

EMMA. Adventure?

MRS. MUKHERJEE. Yes, adventure. You're all going to study a famous explorer, and then present your report at the Swarthmore Library.

MURPHY. The library? My dad says the mayor wants to get rid of it. It has no computers and no Internet, so it's totally busted.

EMMA. It's called World Discovery Day. Maybe there's something in the library we don't know about.

MRS. MUKHERJEE. There's more. We're all going to vote. And whoever has the best report will win a coupon for a free pizza from Renato's! Now, this project's going to be an opportunity for all of you to be very creative…

(A shift.)

So, here are the rules.

ON INDEX CARDS OF SIX BY FOUR
LIST FORTY SEPARATE FACTS OR MORE
INCLUDE YOUR SOURCES
YOU'LL NEED TEN
THAT OUTLINE WHO AND WHAT AND WHEN

YOU'LL BE ALLOWED ONE VISUAL AID
WHERE MAPS AND PICTURES ARE DISPLAYED
THE ART COMPONENT OF YOUR GRADE
BUT THERE ARE RULES ON HOW IT'S MADE

Is everyone taking notes?

(She pulls out an example: a fairly boring-looking poster that says "LEWIS AND CLARK.")

THEY ALL MUST BE THIS SIZE AND SHAPE
NO GLITTER GLUE OR PACKING TAPE
AND IF THEY'RE WHITE, THEY'RE BETTER SEEN
USE PRE-CUT LETTERS SO IT'S CLEAN

SPACE EVERY PICTURE AS IT'S GLUED
SO ALL OF THEM ARE CLEARLY VIEWED
AND LASTLY, FRIENDS, I MUST CONCLUDE
THAT THERE ARE RULES –

EMMA. This doesn't sound like an adventure at all.

MRS. MUKHERJEE. The adventure is in doing it right.

THERE ARE RULES THAT MUST BE FOLLOWED
AND THESE RULES SHOULD BE YOUR FRIEND
THESE RULES CAN BE YOUR PATHWAY TO AN ENVIABLE END
AND RULES EXTEND BEYOND THIS CLASSROOM
LET THEM BE YOUR TOOLS
YOU WILL BEST BE SERVED IF YOU FOLLOW THE RULES

MRS. MUKHERJEE. Now, here is how I want you to outline your explorer's biography. Start with where they were born and then…

(**MRS. MUKHERJEE**'s *voice drifts away as* **EMMA** *daydreams…*)

EMMA.

CAN'T YOU SEE THAT A POSTER BOARD IS BORING?
AND A STORY CAN'T BE TOLD IN BLACK AND GREY?
JUST YOU WAIT
'TIL I TELL MY STORY
ON WORLD DISCOVERY DAY

I'M THE ONE HERE WHO KNOWS ABOUT EXPLORING
I CAN SPOT A NEW ADVENTURE RIGHT AWAY
JUST YOU WAIT
I'LL GIVE YOU ADVENTURE
ON WORLD DISCOVERY DAY

AND OH, I CAN SEE YOUR EYES
AND OH, THEY'LL BE ON ME
AND OH, IMAGINE YOUR SURPRISE
AS YOU REALIZE
HOW AMAZING I CAN BE!

I'LL SHOW YOU THE EXCITEMENT YOU'RE IGNORING
WHEN I FINALLY GET THE CHANCE TO HAVE MY SAY
SO, JUST YOU WAIT
'TIL I HAVE MY MOMENT
ON WORLD DISCOVERY DAY

(**MRS. MUKHERJEE** *walks around the class with a large sombrero.*)

MRS. MUKHERJEE. All right. Now, everyone reach into my hat, one at a time please, and pick your explorer.

SEBBY. (*Looking at his paper*) Admiral Peary! I've got Admiral Peary!

SIMON. Neil Armstrong!

MURPHY. (*Pronounces it with a hard "G"*) Who's Magellan?

NIKKI. Yes! Christopher Columbus!

ZINZI. I've got Sacajawea. Who do you have, Emma?

EMMA. Erik the Red… fox.

NIKKI. What? Who's Erik the Red Fox?

MRS. MUKHERJEE. Erik the Red. Viking Explorer. This could turn out to be the most exciting report in class.

EMMA. Really?

MRS. MUKHERJEE. See Mr. Sigurd in the library. You won't be sorry.

(**EMMA** *retreats into her fantasy again as the classroom,* **KIDS** *and* **MRS. MUKHERJEE** *disappear.*)

EMMA.

OH! I'LL SHOW YOU THE EXCITEMENT YOU'RE IGNORING
WHEN I FINALLY GET THE CHANCE TO HAVE MY SAY
AND JUST YOU WAIT
NOTHING'S GONNA THROW ME
I'LL BE GREAT
NOTHING'S GONNA SLOW ME
SO, JUST YOU WAIT
FINALLY YOU'LL KNOW ME
ON WORLD DISCOVERY DAY
ON WORLD DISCOVERY DAY
ON WORLD DISCOVERY DAY

(**EMMA** *looks at the slip of paper and triumphantly punches the air.*)

MUSIC NO. 4:
"WORLD DISCOVERY DAY PLAY-OFF"

(*The scene segues to…*)

SCENE TWO – INT. A SCHOOL HALLWAY

(OLLIE *meets* EMMA *after class.* EMMA *has kept her fox outfit on.*)

OLLIE. Hewow sistew.

NIKKI. Emma, are you hanging out with a kindergartner?

ZINZI. He's her brother.

NIKKI. Zinzi!

(She makes a "Zip it" gesture. Then, to **EMMA:***)*

Good luck with your World Discovery Day report. It was nice of Mrs. Mukherjee to say it might be good.

EMMA. It will be.

NIKKI. Mm-hmm. See ya...

*(***NIKKI*** exits and* **ZINZI** *follows.*)

OLLIE. What's a wowd discovewy day wepewt?

EMMA. Something awesome. And I've gotta work on it right away. Ollie, we're going to the library.

*(***EMMA*** grabs a phone off a nearby desk and dials.*)

OLLIE. Da Wibwaywie? But we'w be wate fow dinnew! Mom said aftew school, gwab Emma and wun stwait home. No cwazy stuff.

(In another area, we see INT. EMMA'S HOUSE. **MOM** *answers the phone while preparing dinner.*)

MOM. Hello?

EMMA. Mom. Ollie and I are going to the library. Okay?

MOM. Emma? Where are you calling from?

EMMA. The office. Mrs. Pinsker's not at her desk, so I thought...

MOM. Hang up and come home, Emma.

EMMA. But this is important. I have to talk to Mr. Sigurd.

MOM. Who's Mr. Sigurd?

EMMA. You know, the guy who works in the library.

OLLIE. Da wybwawian...

EMMA. Yeah, the librarian. I'll be quick. Promise.

MOM. Emma, I'm going to have dinner ready.

OLLIE. Say it's fow da wepewt.

EMMA. But I *have* to go to the library!

MOM. I'm sure. The same way you *had* to go to the co-op and hide in the produce aisle.

EMMA. I was on safari!

MOM. Emma, come home. I don't have time for "Emma adventures" today.

OLLIE. Say it's fow da wepewt!

EMMA. Dad would let me go.

MOM. Now, that's not fair. I miss your dad just as much as you do when he's working –

EMMA. Adventuring.

MOM. He's *working.* In an office.

EMMA. In North Carolina! He flies in an airplane TWO times a week –

MOM. ENOUGH. HOME. NOW.

OLLIE. *(Exasperated)* Say it's fow da wepewt!!

EMMA. *(Blurting it out)* It's for a report! For school. That's why I want to go to the library. And this report could be the most exciting one in the whole class, Mom!

MOM. *(After a beat)* You swear it's homework and no crazy stuff?

EMMA. On my fuzzy red ears.

MOM. Okay.

EMMA. *(To* **OLLIE***:)* YES! I knew I should have told her about the report!

(**OLLIE** *puts his head in his hands.*)

MOM. But go to the library and ONLY the library. And Emma...hello?

(*But* **EMMA** *has already hung up the phone and pulled* **OLLIE** *offstage.* **MOM** *disappears as the scene shifts to...*)

MUSIC NO. 5:
"THE LIBRARY"

SCENE THREE – INT. LIBRARY

(*The place seems deserted.* **EMMA** *and* **OLLIE** *investigate.*)

EMMA. Crazy. Look at all these books.

OLLIE. Dat's a wot o' books...

EMMA. Hello? Hello? Is anybody here?

SIGURD. *(Appearing)* That depends on who's looking.

(*He examines her.*)

Hmmm. Judging by the pointed rusty-colored ears and the bushy tail, I would have to assume that you're a red fox, also known as *Vulpes vulpes fulvus*. You don't look Tibetan, so I'd say you were native to the North American region. Correct?

EMMA. Whoa.

SIGURD. You're the first of your kind to set foot in my library.

EMMA. Are you –?

SIGURD. Sigurd Torvaldsson. Keeper of the Books. You can call me Mr. Sigurd. And you are?

EMMA. Emma. Keeper of...my brother, Ollie.

OLLIE. I'm hew bwovew.

SIGURD. I see. Well, we don't normally allow wild animals...

EMMA. *(She removes the ears)* Oh, no. I'm no good at being a fox, anyway. I was told to see you.

SIGURD. Huh. Not a lot of folks come through here anymore. These poor books are getting lonely. What is it you're looking for?

EMMA. I need to know about the Vikings.

SIGURD. Vikings?

EMMA. See, I have this report and I...

SIGURD. *(Already searching for books)* Let's see, here. Ancient Romans, Saxons, Samurai... Aha. Read at your own risk.

(*He hands her books.*)

SIGURD. *(cont.) Secrets of the Longboat. Ancient Runes. Norse Mythology: The Book of Gods and Monsters.*

EMMA. Monsters? What do Vikings have to do with –

SIGURD. Everything. At the edge of the world, where the seas end, lays Jotenheim, the land inhabited by enormous Frost Giants.

OLLIE. Fwost Giants?

SIGURD. And Odin, King of the Viking Gods, is the only one who can save you from their wrath. He sold his eye to a witch in order to learn black magic.
(**EMMA** *gasps. An abrupt shift.*)
Nothing super-interesting. Well, I'll leave you to –

EMMA. Wait. Tell me more. Please.

SIGURD. *(He hands her another book.)* There's plenty to read.

EMMA. *(Reading) Erik the Red: A Biography in Blood.* That's my report!

OLLIE. Bwud?!?

SIGURD. *(He hands her another book.) The Vikings: A History.*

MUSIC NO. 6:
"INTO THE STORM"

(Seeing **EMMA** *opening the book:)*

I wouldn't open that if I were you. Not unless you're ready. Books hold enormous power, Emma. They can suck you into a veritable maelstrom of words and images, thoughts, and emotions…

HEAR THEM NOW AS THEY CALL THROUGH AGES
WHISPERING: "I'M A VIKING"
HEAR THEM CALL THROUGH THE INK ON THESE PAGES:
"I AM A FEARSOME VIKING!"

CAN'T YOU HEAR THEIR CRY, SLICING THROUGH THE SKY?
HEAR THEM SHAKE YOU AS THEY TAKE YOU
INTO THE STORM

HERE THEY COME, DO YOU THINK THAT YOU'RE READY?
HOW WILL YOU FACE A VIKING?
FEEL THEIR PULL, ARE YOU HOLDING ON STEADY?

NOTHING STOPS A VIKING…

(**SIGURD** *exits.*)

EMMA. *(Reading, simultaneous with* **VIKINGS***)* "985 A.D. They came from the North. Vikings were advanced shipbuilders, superb sailors and fearless explorers. Known for the carvings of ferocious beasts on the prows of their slender sailing ships, they navigated their vessels through dangerous, uncharted waters!"

(The library is invaded by Norsemen.)

VIKINGS.

AAH! AAH! AAH! AAH!

GENT VIKINGS.

I SEEK THRILLS AND I LIVE TO CHASE GLORY
I AM ONE FINE VIKING!
I DRINK MEAD AND I TELL A GOOD STORY
I AM A FEARSOME VIKING!
WITH MY SWORD AND SHIELD, NEVER WILL I YIELD
THOUGH IT'S HAILING I KEEP SAILING INTO THE STORM
I AM ROUGH AND MY VOICE IS LIKE THUNDER
I AM ONE FINE VIKING!
HEAR ME ROAR AS I PILLAGE AND PLUNDER
I AM A FEARSOME VIKING!

LADY VIKINGS.

I HAVE AN URGE TO EXPLORE
FROM THE MOUNTAINS TO THE SHORE
I'M A DARING AND ADVENTUROUS VIKING
I CHALLENGE EV'RY FRONTIER
AS I TRAVEL FAR AND NEAR
NEVER SATISFIED, I ALWAYS WANT MORE!

LADY VIKINGS	**GENT VIKINGS**

ODIN, BE MY GUIDE

RIDING BY MY SIDE

STRENGTHEN ME AS I AM
FLEEING INTO THE
STORM!

LADY VIKINGS.
I'M IN A CLAN AND I'M
PROUD
TO BE COUNTED IN THEIR
CROWD
I'M A DARING AND
ADVENTUROUS VIKING
HO! HO! HA! HA!

ODIN, BE MY GUIDE

RIDING BY MY SIDE
STRENGTHEN ME AS I AM
FLEEING INTO THE
STORM!

GENT VIKINGS.
HO! HO! HO! HO!

I AM AMAZINGLY STRONG
FOR I KNOW WHERE I
BELONG
AND I'M NOT AFRAID TO
SHOUT IT OUT LOUD!

BOTHVAR. (*Grabbing* **EMMA**) Ah-ha! Look what we've got here, Bone-Threaders! Feisty!

EMMA. Shh! This is a library!

GUNNHILD. (*Tossing* **BOTHVAR** *the book*) Bothvar! Look.

BOTHVAR. Ah. She's been reading!

THORKLE. Then *she* summoned us.

EMMA. I did?

BOTHVAR. Pair an inventive mind with a book…happens every time. So they call you Erma?

EMMA. Emma.

BOTHVAR. Sure. Whatever.

EMMA. And this is my brother, Ollie.

OLLIE. Hewow.

OLAF. Could she be the one we seek?

EMMA. What one?

BOTHVAR. We're looking for a chieftain. A leader. Erik the Red has deserted us in search of Golden Amulets in the Enchanted Fjords. We need someone with a plan. An adventurer.

EMMA. Yes. Yes! That's me!

BOTHVAR. Not so fast. Look at you. You don't have what it takes.

BOTHVAR.

A VIKING'S TOUGH, AND I AINT BRAGGIN'
NOT ONE VIKING'S EVER CRIED
IF YOU WERE NEAR AN ANGRY DRAGON
I THINK YOU'D BE TOAST
A VIKING BATTLES TROLLS AND GIANTS
EVIL WE DO NOT ABIDE
YOU'D SURELY HIDE WHEN SWORDS COLLIDE,
OR POORLY FIGHT AT MOST!

VIKINGS.

A VIKING MUST BE LION-HEARTED
VIKINGS SHOULD BE WILD AND FREE
IF YOU SET SAIL FOR LANDS UNCHARTED
YOU WOULD GO ASTRAY
A VIKING LOVES THE OPEN WATER
VIKINGS HAVE TO KNOW THE SEA
IF YOU ASK ME, I BET YOU'D FLEE
AND LET US LOSE OUR WAY!

YOU DON'T HAVE THE WILL, YOU DON'T HAVE THE SKILL
YOU WON'T LEAD AS WE'RE PROCEEDING
INTO THE STORM! INTO THE STORM!
INTO THE STORM! INTO THE STORM!
INTO THE STORM! INTO THE STORM!

VIKINGS LIKE THRILLS, VIKINGS LIVE TO CHASE GLORY
YOU ARE NOT ONE FINE VIKING!
VIKINGS DRINK MEAD, VIKINGS TELL A GOOD STORY
YOU'RE NOT A FEARSOME VIKING!

(They sing in counterpoint.)

GENT VIKINGS. *(Simultaneous with* **LADIES***)*

VIKINGS LIKE THRILLS, VIKINGS LIVE TO CHASE GLORY
YOU ARE NOT ONE FINE VIKING!
VIKINGS DRINK MEAD, VIKINGS TELL A GOOD STORY
YOU'RE NOT A FEARSOME VIKING!

LADY VIKINGS. *(Simultaneous with* **GENTS***)*
>YOU HAVE NO URGE TO EXPLORE
>FROM THE MOUNTAINS TO THE SHORE
>YOU ARE NOT A TRUE, ADVENTUROUS VIKING
>YOU'LL NEVER FIND A FRONTIER
>AS YOU TRAVEL FAR AND NEAR
>AND YOU'LL NEVER EVER YEARN TO HAVE MORE!

VIKINGS. *(In unison)*
>EMMA, YOU CAN'T LEAD US INTO THE STORM!

(An enormous thunderclap buttons the number.)

EMMA. That's not fair! If I summoned you here, why can't I be your leader?

HELGA. 'cuz you're just a kid with a book.

OLAF. Well said. You haven't earned it.

EMMA. But I'm an adventurer like you've wanted. And I know I could be a great chieftain!

GUNNHILD. Forget it. It'll never happen.

OLLIE. Why not? Give hew a chance, guys. Wet hew pwove it!

BOTHVAR. I have no idea what that kid just said, but I like his spirit.

EMMA. He said let me prove it to you. He's right. If you would just give me a chance, I promise that I'll show you that I can be your leader.

BOTHVAR. Hmm. It won't be easy. You'll be judged by the whole clan. Gunnhild, the She-Bear…

*(***GUNNHILD*** poses and grunts.)*

Olaf, the Boorish…

*(***OLAF*** poses and grunts.)*

Helga, the Clang-Fist…

*(***HELGA*** poses and grunts.)*

Thorkle, the Traveler…

THORKLE. I don't do any of the scary stuff. I'm just well-traveled.

BOTHVAR. And all the others. I'll be the biggest judge of all. They call me Bothvar, the Fork-Splitter!

(All pose and grunt.)

Now, first you'll need a name to prove your Vikinghood. But most importantly, you'll need to show us you can lead a clan of your own.

EMMA. A clan? Where'm I s'posed to get a clan from?

GUNNHILD. Gather your teachers…

HELGA. Your classmates…

BOTHVAR. Your family! Get them to follow you. Look up to you. Like you. Then…we'll see if you're worthy of leading us.

HELGA. We need a chieftain by the half moon. That's –

THORKLE. May 4th.

EMMA. World Discovery Day.

BOTHVAR. If you haven't proven yourself by then…the library is closing.

EMMA. What?

*(**SIGURD** enters and the **VIKINGS** retreat into the shadows.)*

SIGURD. I said the library is closing. What do you think? Of the books? You've had your head in that one for hours.

EMMA. It seemed so real.

SIGURD. You can take it home if you like.

EMMA. How about all of them?

SIGURD. I like you, Emma.

(He exits.)

MUSIC NO. 7:
"EMMA THE RED"

EMMA.
I HAVE WAITED, I HAVE WONDERED
WHEN WILL ADVENTURE FIND ME?
NOW I HEAR IT, WHISPERING SOFTLY

NOW I KNOW WHO I CAN BE...

FEARLESS AND DEFIANT
WITH A HELMET ON MY HEAD
I'LL FACE ANY GIANT
AND HE'LL QUIVER AND SHIVER WITH DREAD
E'VRY TROLL IN A HOLE
WILL BE ROLLING WITH FEAR WHERE I TREAD
I'LL BE MIGHTY EMMA
AWESOME EMMA THE RED!

VIKINGS.

HAUOO! HAUOO! HAUOO!

EMMA.

HELMET? I CAN MAKE IT
WITH SOME FELT, SOME FOIL AND THREAD
ARMOR? I CAN FAKE IT
MAKE A SWORD FROM A BOARD IN THE SHED
AND A CAPE I CAN SHAPE
FROM A DRAPE OR A SHEET FROM MY BED
I'LL BE BRAVEST EMMA
FEARSOME EMMA THE RED

VIKINGS.

HAUOO-AHH!

EMMA.

CAN'T YOU SEE ME SAILING BY,
ON A VIKING SEA?
UNDERNEATH THE NORTHERN SKY
SCHOOL AND CHORES BEHIND ME
SO THERE'S NOTHING THERE TO BIND ME
IF YOU FIND ME, YOU'LL FIND THAT I'M FREE!

VIKINGS.

OH, HAUOO! HAUOO! ETC...

EMMA.

DANGER, HEAR ME CALLING
HAVE YOU HEARD EACH WORD I'VE SAID?
NO WAY AM I STALLING
'CUZ I YEARN FOR THE JOURNEY AHEAD
AND I KNOW AS I GO
HIGH AND LOW, MANY TALES WILL BE SPREAD

OF THE VIKING EMMA,
FIERY EMMA THE RED

VIKINGS.

HAUOO-AHH! OOH. ETC…

EMMA.

CAN'T YOU SEE ME SAILING BY
WATERS FAR FROM TAME?
OVERHEAD THE RAVENS FLY
CAN'T YOU FEEL THE WONDER
OF THE MAGIC SPELL I'M UNDER
AS THE THUNDER IS CALLING MY NAME?

VIKINGS.

DANGER, SHE IS CALLING
HAVE YOU HEARD EACH WORD SHE SAID?

EMMA.

NO WAY AM I STALLING
'CUZ I YEARN FOR THE JOURNEY AHEAD

VIKINGS.

SHE'S NO LONGER SOME TYKE
ON A BIKE, SHE'S A VIKING INSTEAD!
SHE IS MIGHTY EMMA, AWESOME EMMA
DAUNTLESS EMMA, FIERY EMMA
FEARLESS EMMA

EMMA.

DARING EMMA THE RED!

VIKINGS.

HAUOO! HAUOO! HAUOO!

(Blackout.)

MUSIC NO. 8:
"EMMA THE RED PLAY-OFF"

(The scene segues to…)

SCENE FOUR – INT. EMMA'S HOUSE

(**MOM** *is on the phone with Emma's dad.*)

MOM. Dan – Sweetie, I'm telling you, it was like a different child. When you left on Monday, she was in full fox mode. But then last night…all these books. And she just sat there so quietly. I mean, the girl was transfixed. And she was wearing her sweatpants and her Renato's Pizza tee-shirt. I haven't seen her in normal clothes since… Right? Imagine. No more costumes in public, no more scenes…maybe all we had to do was get her a library card. Her report? Well, it's about…

(**OLLIE** *enters with a sheet around his neck and a colander on his head.*)

OLLIE. Biking, Biking, Biking, Biking…

MOM. …Vikings. Oh, God. He probably dressed up himself. Emma's gonna come down here in a nice pair of jeans and…

EMMA. *(Entering in Viking attire)* Morning, Bone-Threaders! Adventure awaits!

MOM. Dan, I gotta go.

(**MOM** *hangs up the phone.*)

EMMA. Well, you look as if you've seen a troll. Haven't you ever been in the presence of a real-live Viking before?

OLLIE. She's a Biking.

EMMA. Not only a Viking, but a Viking who may become chieftain! You may henceforth refer to me as Emma the Red, Viking Explorer.

(**EMMA** *hands* **MOM** *a stone.*)

Here you are, my good woman.

OLLIE. It's a woon.

EMMA. That's pronounced *rune,* my young apprentice.

(To **MOM***:)*

And may it bring you strength. I leave with the tide.

MUSIC NO. 9:
"EMMA GOES TO SCHOOL"

EMMA. *(cont.)* May the Norwegian sun shine upon you! AND LONG LIVE ODIN!

(She exits as the scene shifts…)

SCENE FIVE –
INT. MRS. MUKHERJEE'S CLASSROOM

(**MRS. MUKHERJEE** *settles the kids.*)

MRS. MUKHERJEE. Friends, please be seated as I take roll. Murphy Bean?

MURPHY. Here.

MRS. MUKHERJEE. Ferdinand-Muñoz Twins?

ZINZI & SEBBY. Present!

MRS. MUKHERJEE. Nikki Tibbles?

NIKKI. I worked on my report all night last night, Mrs. Mukherjee.

MRS. MUKHERJEE. Good! Emma Katz?… Emma? Emma Katz are you here?

EMMA. *(Entering)* She most certainly is not!

GUNTHER. Oh, man.

EMMA. I know not of this Emma Katz. I, my friends, am Emma the Red. Warrior. Explorer. Viking. At your service.

MRS. MUKHERJEE. Emma. Emma, this is…

EMMA. Isn't it stirring? I have found my true calling. And it's all thanks to you, Fair Teacher.

(Addressing the room:)

Everyone. I shall be a Viking from this day forth. No more foxes or monkfish or winter squash. And by World Discovery Day, if I can prove myself worthy, I shall be a chieftain. But to do that, I will need as many of you who are brave enough to follow me and look to me as your fearless, yet humble leader. So, who's with me? Who will join my clan?

NIKKI. What in the world was in your Lucky Charms this morning?

MRS. MUKHERJEE. That's enough, Emma. Sit down.

EMMA. Oh, come on! Don't you want to pillage and plunder under the amazing leadership of Emma the Red?

MRS. MUKHERJEE. Emma Katz! You are wasting my valuable time. That's a strike.

(Writes "Emma – 1" *on the board)*

Two more and you sit in the hallway during recess. This classroom can't take any more of your… your…

MURPHY. Shenanigans!… Don't know what it means. My dad just says it when he's mad.

EMMA. It's a fine Viking name. From now on, Murphy Bean, I shall call you Shenanigans the Terrible!

NIKKI. *(To* ZINZI*)* She's lost her mind.

EMMA. I heard that. Have at thee, foul villain!

*(*EMMA *rushes* NIKKI. *The class erupts in chaos.)*

MRS. MUKHERJEE. THAT'S ENOUGH! Everyone needs to settle down. NOW.

(To EMMA, *marking a 2nd strike:)*

That's two strikes. Emma, I am so disappointed in your behavior. You don't listen.

EMMA. I listened to everything you said. I went to the library and learned all this awesome stuff from Mr. Sigurd! Just ask him.

MURPHY. Mr. Sigurd? The old weirdo who works at the dumb library?

SIGURD. *(Entering with a cart of books)* The very same.

MRS. MUKHERJEE. Uh, friends, this is Mr. Sigurd. World Discovery Day is in three short weeks and I thought, since it's being held at his library, that he might come in and help with your research.

*(*ZINZI *raises her hand.)*

Yes, Zinzi?

ZINZI. Why aren't we just having it here?

MRS. MUKHERJEE. Well, because I want to introduce you to a very important place in Swarthmore's history. A place that might not always –

SIGURD. It will, Mrs. Mukherjee. The library will always be available to you children and your families…

MURPHY. Do I need to go to the library if I can just use the computer at my dad's house?

SIGURD. Hmm. Well, I suppose you don't need to. What explorer are you researching?

MURPHY. *(Pronounces it with a hard "G")* Me? Ferdinand Magellan.

SIGURD. *(Correcting, overlapping)* Magellan. Mm-hm.

MURPHY. He's kind of boring. This website said he was born in Spain.

SIGURD. Portugal.

MURPHY. In 14 something.

SIGURD. 1480, right.

MURPHY. Yeah. And he did some kind of circum –

SIGURD. *(Interrupts!)* Circumnavigation.

MURPHY. Yup. Whatever that means.

MUSIC NO. 10:
"KEEP ON SAILING"

SIGURD. It means he was the first person to sail completely around the earth. You mean to tell me you don't know the story of how he proved the earth wasn't flat?

FERDINAND HAD THE WHOLE THING PLANNED
HE WOULD SHOW THE KING THE PLANET WAS ROUND
SAID: "I'LL SWOOP IN A GREAT BIG LOOP
AND I'LL DOCUMENT THE PATH I'VE FOUND"
BUT THE KING SAID: "THE EARTH DOESN'T BEND
AND YOU'LL SAIL STRAIGHT OFF OF THE END!"
DID MAGELLAN CRY AND SHRUG AND SIGH?
OR THINK: "WE'LL SEE, MY FRIEND"?
HE SAID: "KING, I'M GLAD WE COULD CHAT
BUT I'M LEAVING NOW AND THAT'S THAT"
AND DID HE ASTOUND AS HE SAILED 'ROUND?
WELL, HE KNOCKED THAT KING DOWN FLAT!

HE SAID, KEEP ON SAILING
HANG ON THROUGH THE RAIN AND WE'LL FIND OUR WAY
KEEP ON SAILING AND WE'LL MAKE IT THERE SOMEDAY

> IF WE KEEP ON GOIN' WITH NO SIGNS OF SLOWIN'
> THEN IT'S ALL GONNA BE OKAY
> SO UNTIL OUR TROUBLES ARE GONE
> WE KEEP SAILING ON!

MURPHY. That's so cool!

SIGURD. And there's more where that came from.

SEBBY. Mr. Sigurd! Mr. Sigurd! What do you know about Admiral Peary?

SIGURD. Oh, I'm going to need some volunteers for this one!

KIDS. (*Ad lib*) Ooh! Me! Me! Etc.

> (**SIGURD** *organizes the* **KIDS** *to help tell the story.*)

SIGURD.

> PEARY'S GOAL WAS TO REACH THE NORTH POLE
> THOUGH HE KNEW IT WAS A TREACHEROUS TRIP
> SAILED THE BLUE WITH A SHIP AND CREW
> THROUGH THE OCEAN WITH HER ICY GRIP
> WELL, THE SKIES GOT CLOUDY AND GRAY
> AND A STORM BLEW OUR HERO ASTRAY
> WAS HE IN A FUNK? DID HE SAY: "WE'RE SUNK!"
> OR FIND SOME ANOTHER WAY?
> HE SAID: "BOYS, LET'S TRY IT ONCE MORE
> THAT'S WHAT SECOND CHANCES ARE FOR"
> SO, HE SMILED AND THEN HE SAILED AGAIN
> AND HE FOUND THAT ARCTIC SHORE!

SIGURD & KIDS.

> HE SAID, KEEP ON SAILING
> HANG ON THROUGH THE RAIN AND WE'LL FIND OUR WAY
> KEEP ON SAILING AND WE'LL MAKE IT THERE SOMEDAY
> IF WE KEEP ON GOIN'
> WITH NO SIGNS OF SLOWIN'
> THEN IT'S ALL GONNA BE OKAY
> SO UNTIL OUR TROUBLES ARE GONE
> WE KEEP SAILING ON!
>
> KEEP ON SAILING! KEEP ON SAILING! SAIL ON!
> KEEP ON SAILING! KEEP ON SAILING! SAIL ON!

NIKKI. Mr. Sigurd, I have Christopher Columbus!

SIGURD. *(Tosses her a book)* Then you'll need *Italian Explorers 101*.

PHYLLIS. I've got Sir Francis Drake.

SIGURD. *(Tossing a book)* Did you know he was a pirate?

(He crosses to **EMMA**.*)*

Ah. And I know this young Viking has Erik the Red. What story should we tell?

EMMA. The one where he got kicked out of Iceland? Or when he discovered Greenland? Or when –

SIGURD. Seems you know them all. But do you know the tale of the Viking, Harald Fairhair?

HARALD FAIR HAD A GREAT HEAD OF HAIR
HE WAS HOPIN' IT WOULD WIN HIM A BRIDE

KIDS.

WIN HIM A BRIDE!

SIGURD.

SAID: "I'LL WOO PRINCESS GYDA THE BLUE
FOR SHE MAKES ME FEEL ALL GUSHY INSIDE"

KIDS.

EW! GROSS!

SIGURD.

BUT THEN, GYDA SAID: "KID, HERE'S THE THING …"

KIDS.

WHAT? WHAT?

SIGURD.

"… YOU'LL NEVER WED ME UNLESS YOU'RE A KING"

KIDS.

OH, NO!

SIGURD.

DID THAT WEAR HIM THIN? DID HE JUST GIVE IN?
OR BUY THAT DIAMOND RING?

KIDS.

TELL US! OOH!

SIGURD.

> HE SAID: "PRINCESS, I THINK THAT'S FAIR
> 'TIL I'M KING, I WON'T CUT MY HAIR"
> SO, HE SAILED ALONE AND SEIZED A THRONE
> WITH HAIR BEYOND COMPARE!

SIGURD & KIDS.

> HE SAID, KEEP ON SAILING
> HANG ON THROUGH THE RAIN AND WE'LL FIND OUR WAY
> OH! KEEP ON SAILING!
> AND WE'LL MAKE IT THERE SOMEDAY!
> IF WE KEEP ON GOIN' WITH NO SIGNS OF SLOWIN'
> THEN IT'S ALL GONNA BE OKAY
> SO UNTIL OUR TROUBLES ARE GONE
> WE KEEP SAILING ON!
>
> KEEP ON SAILING!
> HANG ON THROUGH THE RAIN AND WE'LL FIND OUR WAY
> KEEP ON SAILING AND WE'LL MAKE IT THERE SOMEDAY
> IF WE KEEP ON GOIN' WITH NO SIGNS OF SLOWIN'
> THEN IT'S ALL GONNA BE OKAY
> SO UNTIL OUR TROUBLES ARE GONE
> UNTIL OUR TROUBLES ARE GONE
> UNTIL OUR TROUBLES ARE GONE
> WE KEEP SAILING ON!
>
> KEEP ON SAILING! KEEP ON SAILING! KEEP ON SAILING!
> KEEP ON SAILING! KEEP ON SAILING! SAILING ON!

(The song buttons for applause, then revs up again.)

SIGURD & KIDS.

> KEEP ON SAILING!
> HANG ON THROUGH THE RAIN AND WE'LL FIND OUR WAY
> KEEP ON SAILING AND WE'LL MAKE IT THERE SOMEDAY
> IF WE –

EMMA. Yes! *Yes!* Yo-Ho! *Vikings!*!! Yo, Vikings!

*(**EMMA** brandishes a sword. The music falls apart and the singing fades into stunned silence.)*

MRS. MUKHERJEE. Emma! Give me that sword. Now.

EMMA. But we're telling Viking stories! I have a ton of 'em. Oh man, you guys'll totally wanna join my clan once you hear these!

MRS. MUKHERJEE. Three strikes. Out. OUT. Out of my classroom!

(The bell rings. **KIDS** *scatter.* **MUKHERJEE** *grabs* **EMMA** *and plops her in the hallway.)*

You always take it a step too far. If you bring a weapon to class again, I will have to consider suspension. Now, you are going to sit in this hallway until you decide that you're truly ready to join this class. Do you understand?

*(***MUKHERJEE*** *exits.* **SIGURD** *sits next to* **EMMA.** *)*

MUSIC NO. 11:
"KEEP ON SAILING (REPRISE)"

EMMA. It was just a sword.

SIGURD. Spare the sword. Summon a book.

EMMA. I found my calling. But they'll never believe I can be a Viking. They'll never believe in Vikings at all…

SIGURD.

KEEP ON SAILING
HANG ON THROUGH THE RAIN AND YOU'LL FIND YOUR WAY
KEEP ON SAILING AND YOU'LL MAKE IT THERE SOMEDAY…

But for now, here's something to cheer you up. Proof that Vikings are still around.

(Hands her a clipping.)

AND UNTIL YOUR TROUBLES ARE GONE
YOU KEEP SAILING ON

(He exits.)

EMMA. *(Reading the clipping)* No. Way.

(The scene segues to…)

SCENE SIX – EXT. SCHOOLYARD / JOTUNHEIM

(**OLLIE** *enters.* **EMMA** *runs to him.*)

MUSIC NO. 12 AND 13:
"EMMA THE RED (REPRISE)" and "THE PRAYER"

EMMA. Ollie! You gotta hear this!

OLLIE. No, Emma. We gotta go home. It's macawonie night!

EMMA. It's amazing!

OLLIE. I know! I wuv macawonie!

EMMA. (*Showing him the clipping*) No. No, this. Listen…

(*She reads to him:*)

"Viking Ship for Sale. This 29-foot long boat with a red dragon's head mast was donated by an old Norse woman to the Sons of Valhalla Hall in Asgard, Pennsylvania, and has been on display in our adjacent museum space for over forty years. If not sold, it will be burned. 7000 dollars or best offer. Please contact Ivan Sindri at 549 West Heimdal Street, Asgard, PA!"

OLLIE. A wccw ship? Fow weew?

EMMA. For real.

OLLIE.

I CAN SEE YOU SAIWING BY
ON DA WAVES YOU FWOAT
OBAHEAD DA DWAGONS FWY
AND I GAWANTEE YOU
EVWEEWUN WIW WANNA BE YOU
WHEN DEY SEE YOU ON TOP 'O DAT BOAT!

EMMA.

SOON YOU'LL SEE ME ZOOMIN'
AS I FEED ON MEAD AND BREAD!

OLLIE.

I WIW BE YOW CWEWMAN!
AN A HORN WIW BE WORN ON MY HEAD!

EMMA.

WITH A SPARK WE'LL EMBARK
AND THE DARK OF THE STORM WILL HAVE FLED
WHEN AT LAST I'M EMMA –

OLLIE.

FI-WEE EMMA!

EMMA & OLLIE.

MIGHTY EMMA, AWESOME EMMA!
FEARLESS EMMA!

EMMA.

CHIEFTAIN

EMMA & OLLIE.

EMMA THE RED!

(The **VIKINGS** *invade the schoolyard. As the scene progresses, we are pulled ever deeper into the world of* **EMMA***'s fantasy.)*

BOTHVAR. Not so fast.

EMMA. Bothvar!

BOTHVAR. So we meet again, Erma!

EMMA. Emma.

BOTHVAR. Sure. Whatever. At this rate you'll never be chieftain anyway, so...

EMMA. Why not?

HELGA. How many people did you get to join your clan?

EMMA. Well, I'm still working on that. See...

GUNNHILD. No one. Your teachers...

HELGA. Your classmates...

THORKLE. They laughed at you.

OLAF. They took away your weapon.

BOTHVAR. They basically all told you to get lost. That means you failed, Erma.

VIKINGS. Emma!

BOTHVAR. Sure. Whatever.

EMMA. You have to give me more time. World Discovery Day isn't for another two weeks. I'll win them over.

HELGA. Sure you will.

OLLIE. She wiw! She's gonna get a wong boat wid a dwagonhead ona fwont!

BOTHVAR. What language is this kid speaking? Troll?

EMMA. *(Showing them the paper)* Here. Look at this.

GUNNHILD. *(Grabbing the paper)* Holy Thor's Hammer. She's found herself a ship…

THORKLE. Only true chieftains can obtain their own sailing vessels…

(Two black ravens circle above the **VIKINGS,** *who gasp in awe.)*

BOTHVAR. The ravens! It's a sign.

EMMA. The what?

HELGA. Odin's Ravens. Hugin and Munin. They see and know everything.

GUNNHILD. It's always wise to listen to the wisdom of the birds.

OLLIE. Gotta wisten to da boods, Emma.

BOTHVAR. They rarely show themselves to mortals. This longboat you seek must truly be your destiny.

EMMA. Oh, man! If I can just get it, we'll be sailing with Odin alongside us, riding his eight-legged horse…

OLLIE. A horse wif eight wegs?

OLAF. Brings a tear to my good eye.

EMMA. Then everybody'll have to believe that I'm a real Viking. Won't they?

BOTHVAR. *Won't* they! You must retrieve this vessel.

EMMA. Will you help me?

BOTHVAR. Of course. But first…we pray.

(The **VIKINGS** *kneel.)*

BOTHVAR.

> BIRDS ON HIGH
> GRANT US PEACE OF MIND
> AS WE BEGIN THE ADVENTURE
> HELP US SEE
> SO THAT WE MAY FIND
> THE MEANING OF THE ADVENTURE
>
> MAY WE ENJOY THE JOURNEY
> EVEN IF WE ALL SHOULD FAIL
> BIRDS ON HIGH
> GRANT US CHANGE IN THE WIND
> AND GIVE US THE COURAGE TO SAIL
> GIVE US THE COURAGE TO SAIL

VIKINGS.

> BIRDS ON HIGH
> MAKE THE HARDSHIPS GREAT
> SO WE MAY EARN THE ADVENTURE
> HELP US NOW
> TO ACCEPT OUR FATE
> AS WE TAKE ON THE ADVENTURE
>
> MAY WE EMBRACE THE THUNDER
> SO WE MAY ALL TELL THE TALE
> BIRDS ON HIGH
> GRANT US CHANGE IN THE WIND
> AND GIVE US THE COURAGE TO SAIL
> GIVE US THE COURAGE TO SAIL

(The **VIKINGS** *engage in a ritualistic dance, pulling* **EMMA** *and* **OLLIE** *into their revelry. The ravens flutter overhead.)*

BOTHVAR. Adventure awaits!

MUSIC NO. 14:
"THE ASGARD VESSEL"

BOTHVAR. What say you, birds? What is our course? I see... You're sure?

EMMA. What is it?

BOTHVAR. They say we have to retrieve your ship from the far reaches at the edge of the world: Jotunheim. And those who travel there don't always return.

EMMA. It's worth the risk.

BOTHVAR. Spoken like a true Viking. To the boats. Quickly! Before the storm takes hold.

(*The* **VIKINGS** *board small boats.*)

VIKINGS. (*Singing*)

OH, AH! OH, AH!

(*A terrible, dark storm descends upon the Viking vessels. Lightning flashes, and the seas churn.*)

OLAF. Too late!

BOTHVAR. Hang on!

EMMA. We'll never make it!

HELGA. Never say never, kid!

BOTHVAR. There it is! There's Jotunheim. Through the green mist!

(*The boats crash onto the rocky shore. The* **VIKINGS** *disembark.*)

BOTHVAR. Lanterns.

(*The* **VIKINGS** *comply.*)

EMMA. It's freezing.

GUNNHILD. Shh. You don't want to wake any trolls.

THORKLE. Or giants.

(*A gust of wind extinguishes the lanterns, leaving the* **VIKINGS** *in darkness.*)

OLAF. Uh-oh.

OLLIE. Who tuwned out da wights?

(*We hear giant footsteps.*)

EMMA. What is that?

BOTHVAR. Hold on…

(**BOTHVAR** *reignites his lantern, revealing* **MJÖLVERK**,
an enormous, two-headed frost giant.)

MJÖLVERK (MOM). Who desires my ship?

EMMA. *(To* **BOTHVAR***)* It's enormous!

GUNNHILD. Frost Giants usually are.

EMMA. And with two heads…

MJÖLVERK (MOM). Answer me! Who desires my ship?!?

EMMA. I do. I'm Emma the Red. And I need it to be chieftain.

MJÖLVERK (MOM). You desire what is out of your reach. How much does it cost, dear? How much does it cost to purchase such a ship?

EMMA. Uh…7000 dollars.

MJÖLVERK (MOM). Out of the question! Do you think we're made of money? Do you know how hard we work for you and your brother?

EMMA. What?

MJÖLVERK (MOM). Do you? DO YOU?

EMMA. But…

(*Lights shift to reveal…*)

SCENE SEVEN – INT. EMMA'S HOUSE

(**MOM** *stands over* **EMMA** *and* **OLLIE**.)

MOM. No, really, Emma. Seven thousand dollars is a lot of money. You're looking at me like I have two heads. We can't spend seven thousand dollars on some enormous toy…

EMMA. It's not a toy! Don't you understand? I'm going to be a real-live Viking. I have to get this ship by World Discovery Day to be a chieftain! Mom, please!

OLLIE. Pweese! Pweese!

EMMA. I'll never ask you for anything again. Never ever.

(**EMMA** *makes puppy dog eyes.*)

MOM. Oh, no. Don't. Not "The Look."

MUSIC NO. 15:
"I LOVE YOU, BUT NO"

AS OFTEN AS I PRIDE MYSELF ON GOING WITH THE FLOW
MY DARLING, I'M BESIDE MYSELF
YOU'VE DEALT ME QUITE A BLOW
AND THOUGH I'D LOVE TO BUY THIS VIKING THING
AND TOP IT WITH A BOW
I HAVE TO SAY THAT PHRASE YOU HATE
I LOVE YOU, BUT NO

I LOVE YOU
YOU KNOW THAT I LOVE YOU
YOU KNOW THAT I'D GLADLY GIVE YOU MY LEFT EYE
AND THOUGH YOU ARE DRIVEN
I'M NOT GONNA GIVE IN
YOUR CRAZY REQUEST, AT BEST
CAN ONLY MAKE ME CRY

SO, THERE'S NO NEED FOR SHOUTING, PLEASE
WE'LL BOTH LET THIS ONE GO
AND SPARE ME FROM THE POUTING, PLEASE
(WE KNOW THAT YOU'RE A PRO!)

MOM. *(cont.)*

> AND THOUGH I'M SURE YOU'LL KEEP ME FEELING LIKE
> THE LOWEST OF THE LOW
> I HAVE TO SAY THAT AWFUL PHRASE
> THE ONE THAT KEEPS ME UP FOR DAYS
> AND THOUGH YOU'RE GONNA HATE ME IN A MILLION WAYS
> I LOVE YOU, BUT NO!

> *(**MOM** starts to exit.)*

EMMA. Mom! No! You're ruining everything!

MOM. Emma. Don't test me. This Viking phase has gotten out of hand enough, as it is.

EMMA. It's not a phase. It's real.

MOM. No. No, it is NOT real, Emma. You're not a Viking. None of these adventures with 7000-dollar ships are real. None of them.

> *(**MOM** exits.)*

EMMA. Mom! Mom!!

> *(To **OLLIE**:)*

Now what?

OLLIE. I would give you my Wegos and my favowit teeshewt and da two dowas I got fwom da toofaiwie if dat would help you get yow ship, Emma.

EMMA. Oh, Ollie, that's…that's it. Mr. Sindri's ad said 7000 dollars *or* best offer, right? So, what else can we *offer* him? Ollie, you're brilliant! Could you get my shoebox, please? And a pen!

> *(**OLLIE** grabs a box and brings it to **EMMA**. She dumps its contents on the floor: assorted junk and a piggy bank. She empties the piggy bank and begins to compose a letter.)*

MUSIC NO. 16:
"THE LETTER"

EMMA.

DEAR MR. SINDRI
COULD YOU HELP A VIKING OUT?
WHAT I MEAN IS…
WELL, I HEARD YOU'RE SELLING A LONG BOAT
WITH A REALLY BEAUTIFUL DRAGON HEAD
AND I'D KINDA LIKE TO HAVE IT, PLEASE
FOR SAILING ADVENTURES AND STUFF

NOW, LET'S TALK MONEY
SO YOU'LL GRANT THIS VIKING'S WISH
I'M PREPARED TO OFFER YOU
ONE HUNDRED AND TWENTY-EIGHT DOLLARS
… IN CHANGE
PLUS THREE PHILLIES BASEBALL CARDS

(**EMMA** *thinks better of it and erases that last bit.*)

TWO PHILLIES BASEBALL CARDS

(**OLLIE** *shakes his head.* **EMMA** *erases the word* "TWO."
Then, reluctantly…)

THREE PHILLIES BASEBALL CARDS!
AND A VERY, VERY, VERY, VERY SHARP FOX TOOTH

OH, MR. SINDRI
I'M BEGGING YOU TO HELP THIS VIKING OUT!
AND, WHATEVER YOU DO, DON'T BURN THE BOAT
BEFORE YOU READ THIS LETTER!

LOVE… (NO)
SEALED WITH A KISS… (NO)
SIGNED IN BLOOD INSTEAD! (NO NO NO NO NO…)
SINCERELY, EMMA
EMMA THE RED

(**EMMA** *looks up hopefully. Blackout.*)

MUSIC NO. 17:
"SALLY INTRO ONE"

SCENE EIGHT – EXT. PLAYGROUND

(*Two weeks later. Lights up on* **SEBBY** *and* **MURPHY**.)

SEBBY. So, Mrs. Mukherjee said that Emma's World Discovery Day report could be the best in the class. But Nikki says that (since she has Columbus) that hers'll be the best. But Mr. Sigurd has been helping me a lot with my research, so I think mine might be even better and then maybe I'll win the pizza prize tomorrow! What do you think?

(*A beat. Then* **MURPHY** *belches.*)

MUSIC NO. 18:
"SALLY INTRO TWO"

(**SEBBY** *and* **MURPHY** *exit.* **NIKKI** *and* **ZINZI** *enter.*)

NIKKI. Zinzi, do you have a cupcake in your lunch today?

ZINZI. Yeah. My mom made it. Oh…do you want it?

NIKKI. (*Manipulatively*) Well, I mean, if you don't –

ZINZI. You can have it.

(**ZINZI** *gives* **NIKKI** *the cupcake, sheepishly.*)

NIKKI. Have you seen her yet?

ZINZI. Who?

NIKKI. You know. *Emma.* I just feel bad for her. Gotta look out for the poor thing.

ZINZI. You're really sweet, Nikki.

NIKKI. It's 'cuz her dad's not around that she's so disturbed. That's what I think.

ZINZI. Sure. I hope she does really well at World Discovery Day. Then maybe everybody would –

NIKKI. But she won't. I mean, you don't think she will, do you?

ZINZI. I don't know. Mrs. Mukherjee said her report could be the best in the –

NIKKI. You can't vote for her to win the pizza, Zinzi. Promise me you won't do it.

ZINZI. But I thought you said –

MUSIC NO. 19:
"THE TERRIBLE TALE OF SALLY SHAPIRO"

NIKKI. ZINZI! We can't give Emma any more attention because…well, she might… I shouldn't tell you what she did before.

ZINZI. Why? What did she do?

NIKKI.

DID YOU KNOW SALLY SHAPIRO?

ZINZI.

UH, NO

NIKKI.

SHE WAS A GIRL WHO USED TO GO HERE

ZINZI.

WHEN?

NIKKI.

IT DOESN'T MATTER
YOU KNOW THAT LITTLE PINK MITTEN
THAT'S BEEN SITTIN' IN THE LOST AND FOUND? IT'S HERS
THAT'S ALL THAT'S LEFT OF SHAPIRO

ZINZI.

OH, NO!

NIKKI.

SHE REALLY TOOK AN AWFUL BLOW HERE

ZINZI.

NU-UH!

NIKKI.

UH-HUH! UH-HUH!
'CUZ EMMA SAID SOME STUFF
AND THINGS GOT REALLY ROUGH
AND I CAN'T BE SPECIFIC, BUT IT WAS HORRIFIC
AND SALLY HAD TO TRANSFER TO ANOTHER SCHOOL IN
ALBUQUERQUE!

NIKKI. *(cont)*

THAT'S WHAT SALLY SAID
EVERY SINGLE WORD, I SWEAR
THAT'S WHAT SHE SAID
DON'T BELIEVE ME IF YOU DARE!
SALLY SHAPIRO HAD SO MUCH TO FEAR
OH, SHE'S DAMAGED BEYOND ALL REPAIR!
SHE COULD HAVE WOUND UP DEAD!
WELL, THAT'S WHAT SALLY SAID

But you have to promise me you're not going to tell anybody this, or we're both in danger.

ZINZI. I promise!

(**NIKKI** *exits as* **SEBBY** *enters.*)

Hey, Sebby!

DID YOU KNOW SALLY SHAPIRO?

SEBBY.

UH…

ZINZI.

I GUESS SHE WAS A GIRL WHO WENT HERE

SEBBY.

OH
I NEED A SODA

ZINZI.

LISTEN! SHE HAD A LITTLE PINK KITTEN
THAT'S BEEN SITTIN' IN THE LOST AND FOUND FOR YEARS
YEAH, THAT BELONGED TO SHAPIRO
THAT CAT!

SEBBY.

THAT'S KINDA WEIRD, I NEVER SEEN IT

ZINZI.

SHUT UP! SHUT UP! SHUT UP!
SEE, EMMA STOLE HER STUFF
AND IF THAT WAS NOT ENOUGH
WELL, I DON'T KNOW THE STORY
BUT IT WAS SO GORY THAT

> SALLY WAS PUT IN A MENTAL INSTITUTION…
> IN ALCATRAZABERKEE!

> THAT'S WHAT NIKKI SAID SALLY SAID
> AND NIKKI TIBBLES NEVER LIES
> THAT'S WHAT SHE SAID THAT SHE SAID
> IT SHOULDN'T COME AS SUCH A SURPRISE
> BECAUSE OF THE VIOLENCE
> SHE SWORE ME TO SILENCE
> WITH TEARS COMIN' OUT OF HER EYES!
> THE STORY'S GOT SOME CRED
> IF IT'S WHAT NIKKI SAID

> *(**ZINZI** exits as **MURPHY** enters.)*

SEBBY. *(Crossing to **MURPHY**:)*
> I HEARD THIS GIRL WHO MESSED WITH EMMA
> WOUND UP IN A DILEMMA AND CRIED

MURPHY.
> WHAT'S WRONG WITH CRYING?

SEBBY.
> THERE'S MORE! THEY FOUGHT SINCE THEY WERE BABIES
> BUT THEN EMMA GAVE HER RABIES
> AND SHE TOTALLY DIED!

MURPHY. Woah!

SEBBY.
> THE FACTS ARE THE FACTS
> SO WHEN EMMA ATTACKS
> WELL, I WANT YOU TO KNOW WHAT TO DO
> BECAUSE WHAT ZINZI SAYS NIKKI SAYS SALLY SAYS
> HAS TO BE PROBABLY TRUE

> *(**SEBBY** exits as **NIKKI** enters.)*

MURPHY. Nikki! Oh, man! Nikki, did you hear what happened?

NIKKI. What?

MURPHY. *(Flustered)* Emma… she… The girl…cat… CATS! All murdered! In Berkeeberkeeberkeeville! Can you believe it?!

NIKKI. *(Deeply, deeply satisfied)* Every word.

*(We see all the **KIDS** on their cell phones, singing in counterpoint.)*

MURPHY

PICK UP THE PHONE! PICK UP THE PHONE!
OH MY GOD. YOU GOTTA
PICK UP THE PHONE! PICK UP THE PHONE!

SEBBY.

HEY! HEY DUDE! YOU HAVE TO HEAR THIS!

ZINZI.

SHOULD I CALL 9-1-1? SHOULD I CALL 9-1-1?

NIKKI.

THAT PIZZA IS MINE! THAT PIZZA IS MINE! MINE! MINE!

KIDS. *(In unison)*

AND THAT'S WHAT (SALLY/NIKKI/ZINZI/SEBBY) SAID

MURPHY. That's what somebody said!

I CAN'T BELIEVE SHE LOST HER CAT!

NIKKI.

THAT'S WHAT STANLEY…

ZINZI.

EDWARD…

SEBBY.

GUNTHER…

ALL.

SAID!

MURPHY. Somebody told that to me!

ZINZI.

EMMA HIT HER WITH A BAT

MURPHY, SEBBY & ZINZI.

KNOCKED HER FLAT!

NIKKI.

EMMA, HOW DARE YOU
IT'S REALLY UNFAIR
YOU SHOULD NOT HAVE KILLED SALLY LIKE THAT

KIDS.

> AND THAT'S WHAT SALLY SAID
> THAT'S WHAT NIKKI SAID SALLY SAID!
> THAT'S WHAT…

MURPHY.

> GORDON SAID…

SEBBY.

> SEETHAL SAID…

ZINZI.

> PASHA SAID…

NIKKI.

> MURPHY SAID…

KIDS.

> SEBBY SAID, ZINZI SAID, NIKKI SAID
> SALLY SAID!

MURPHY. Wait, what happened?

(Blackout.)

MUSIC NO. 20:
"SALLY PLAY-OFF"

SCENE NINE: EXT. LIBRARY

(The next day. **MOM** *and* **OLLIE** *ready* **EMMA** *for World Discovery Day.)*

MOM. All right. Big day. Don't forget your poster.

EMMA. I shan't. A chieftain never forgets her supplies.

MOM. Emma…remember what I said about just saying what it is you love about Vikings instead of playing make-believe? I don't want you to make things harder for yourself.

EMMA. The way of a Viking is hard. But you'll see, Mom. It's all going to be ok because when Mr. Sindri sends me that ship…

MOM. Oh, Emma. The ship is out of the question –

EMMA. I wrote him a letter. I offered him my life savings!

MOM. Emma! Emma, you didn't!

(Taken aback by **MOM***'s response,* **EMMA** *bolts into the library.)*

MUSIC NO. 21:
"WORLD DISCOVERY DAY (REPRISE)"

MOM. *(cont.)* Emma, come back!

*(***MOM** *and* **OLLIE** *disappear as the scene immediately segues to… INT. LIBRARY. A banner reads "WORLD DISCOVERY DAY."* **MRS.** **MUKHERJEE** *assembles the* **KIDS.***)*

MRS. MUKHERJEE.
GATHER 'ROUND AND SEE SOMETHING WORTH EXPLORING!
OUR EVENT IS SET TO START WITHOUT DELAY!

KIDS.
I'VE LEARNED A LOT!

MRS. MUKHERJEE.
HOPE IT'S TO YOUR LIKING!

KIDS.
GAVE IT ALL I'VE GOT!

NIKKI.
> I KNOW I'LL BE STRIKING!

EMMA.
> IT'S MY FINAL SHOT
> TO PROVE THAT I'M A VIKING
> ON WORLD DISCOVERY DAY

ALL.
> IT'S WORLD DISCOVERY DAY!
> IT'S WORLD DISCOVERY DAY!

> *(ZINZI has just finished presenting, garnering tepid applause from the students sitting cross-legged in front of her. NIKKI and EMMA are on deck, waiting to the side of the room.)*

MRS. MUKHERJEE. Thank you, Zinzi, for that stirring report on Sacajawea. Next, we have Nikki Tibbles…

NIKKI. *(To EMMA:)* See ya on the other side, weirdo…

MRS. MUKHERJEE. …and her piece on Christopher Columbus.

> *(Tepid applause. NIKKI takes the stage.)*

All right. Emma, you're next.

NIKKI. Who's ever heard someone say "In fourteen hundred ninety-two, Columbus sailed the ocean blue"?

> *(BOTHVAR appears behind EMMA's shoulder.)*

BOTHVAR. This is your last chance, Erma. Has the ship come yet?

EMMA. I promise. It'll be here. I'll prove myself. You'll see.

BOTHVAR. Don't let us down.

> *(SIGURD approaches EMMA and BOTHVAR disappears.)*

SIGURD. Nervous?

EMMA. Huh? Oh. A little.

SIGURD. Remember the story I told you? About the bearded dragon?

EMMA. Nidhogg?

SIGURD. That's the one. And remember, old Nidhogg would feed on people's fear. He could find a way into the heart of a Viking and taunt him. Make him feel worthless.

EMMA. But the dragon slayer stopped him.

SIGURD. Mm-hm. Go out there and slay that dragon, kid.

(He starts off.)

EMMA. Mr. Sigurd.

(She pulls a homemade helmet out of her backpack.)

This is for you. I hereby dub thee Sigurd the Smart: Chieftain of Knowledge, Protector of the Sacred, and Warrior Against Injustice.

SIGURD. I am humbled and most honored.

*(He kneels and **EMMA** places the helmet on his head. Meanwhile, **NIKKI** is finishing her presentation.)*

NIKKI. And that is why Columbus is the best explorer of them all. Because he discovered America. Thank you.

*(Tepid applause. **MRS. MUKHERJEE** takes the stage.)*

MRS. MUKHERJEE. Thank you, Nikki. Now, before our next presenter, I'd just like to remind everyone how wonderful our experience at the library has been these past few weeks. And I urge you to come here with your families more often… It's still a wonderful place to read and learn. And now, Emma Katz.

NIKKI. *(Whispering)* Sit back. She's dangerous.

EMMA. Hello. I am Emma the Red, Viking Explorer…

NIKKI. More like Emma the Weird.

EMMA. …and I'd like to talk to you about a close relation of mine, Mr. Erik the Red.

*(Hearing the **KIDS** giggle:)*

It's true. I'm a Viking. I really am.

MRS. MUKHERJEE. Emma, go on with your report please.

EMMA. No. You can't laugh at me. Stop laughing, Nikki Tibbles! You know what? Christopher Columbus didn't even discover America. Erik the Red and his son Leif discovered it 500 years before Columbus even got there!

NIKKI. That's not true! There's a holiday and everything!

EMMA. I just want to say to all you non-believers out there, that I will be Viking Chieftain whether you like it or not. And I can prove it. Because two weeks ago I wrote a letter to Mr. Ivan Sindri of the Sons of Valhalla Hall asking him for a real-life longboat that he's selling. And I promise you he's going to deliver it here. To Swarthmore. And when he does, you'll all see!

MURPHY. She's so crazy!

SEBBY. She's unstable!

NIKKI. Emma, I don't think you should lie. There's no longboat.

EMMA. There is!

MURPHY. Come on, Emma! For the last time, you're not a Viking. You're my neighbor. We go to the same pool!

(The scene at the library becomes surreal. Everyone circles **EMMA***, voices distorted. They grab materials from their World Discovery Day reports: cardboard boxes, pieces of fabric, wooden dowels, backpacks, flashlights, etc. Eventually, the pieces swirl together to create an enormous, bearded dragon, "NIDHOGG," breathing fire and thunderously flapping his wings.)*

MUSIC NO. 22:
"THE DRAGON SLAYER"

NIKKI. We're tired of your Viking Voodoo, Emma the Weird!

ZINZI. Viking Voodoo!

SEBBY. Viking Voodoo!

EMMA. Back, dragon! Back!

MRS. MUKHERJEE. You will sit in this hallway until you're ready to be a part of the class…

PASHA & PHYLLIS. You'll never be a part of the class…

NIKKI. You'll never be a real Viking…

GUNTHER & SIMON. Emma, you can't wear that to school.

MRS. MUKHERJEE. That's not how a fifth grader behaves.

EMMA. Go away, dragon…go away, dragon….

NIKKI. None of your adventures are real, Emma. None of them!

ZINZI & SEBBY. 'cuz you're just a little girl…

NIKKI. Just a little girl…

MUKHERJEE. Just a little girl…

(**NIDHOGG**, *now fully formed, growls ferociously.*)

ALL (NIDHOGG). *(Terrifyingly)* Just a little girl!!!

(**BOTHVAR** *appears.*)

BOTHVAR. Now you've done it! Run! There's no way you can fight Nidhogg. He'll chew you up and spit you out! Run while you still can.

EMMA. I have to show him! I have to prove to him that –

(**NIDHOGG** *lets out a growl.*)

Help! Sigurd the Smart! Help! Help!!

(**SIGURD** *enters in a tunic and helmet, with sword and shield. He does battle with* **NIDHOGG.**)

SIGURD. Back! Back, you foul beast!

(Swings at the dragon.)

Emma is a true Viking in spirit!

(A blow.)

Vikings are honorable!

(A blow.)

Vikings seek knowledge!

(A blow.)

Vikings are true of heart!

(A blow.)

Vikings are worthy friends!

(A blow.)

Vikings… Vikings…

*(**SIGURD** corners the dragon. Just as he is about to give it a final blow, he turns to **EMMA**, winded.)*

EMMA. Please. Get rid of it. Make it go away.

SIGURD. I can't, Emma. I have to stop. I have battles of my own…

EMMA. What?

*(The dragon scatters into pieces and vanishes. **SIGURD** faces front, in real time, addressing everyone in the library.)*

SIGURD. Everyone… I'd like to thank you all for coming to the library today. Although I wish events like World Discovery Day could continue here, unfortunately, the town council has other plans. Money is tight and… we've lost our funding. So, it is with great sadness that I announce my retirement and the closing of a very old institution here in Swarthmore…

EMMA. No.

SIGURD. I thank you for your support over these many years.

EMMA. NO!

SIGURD. I'm sorry, Emma. Sometimes…the dragon wins.

*(He exits. **EMMA** runs downstage, tearing off her helmet and collapsing, devastated. The scene segues to…)*

SCENE TEN –
EXT. A CURB OUTSIDE THE LIBRARY

*(**MOM** enters.)*

MUSIC NO. 23:
"EMMA THE RED (REPRISE 2)"

MOM. Emma?

(Approaching her:)

Emma, what are you doing out here?

EMMA. I'm sorry, all right. I'm sorry I'm crazy. I'm sorry everybody hates me. I'm sorry I ruin everything.

*(**MOM** sits down next to her.)*

Go ahead. Yell at me. I can take it. I can't feel any worse than I feel right now. I'm probably failing school. I have no calling. The library…my library is gone.

MOM. Emma –

EMMA. I couldn't do anything wrong there, you know? No matter what. When I was there, I was…liked.

MOM. And you weren't liked at home? I like you.

EMMA. Do you?

MOM. *(Beat, a realization:)* Oh, Emma… I love you. So much…

EMMA. But I make it hard. And I mess things up. I could have saved Mr. Sigurd and the books if I had known…

MOM. There was nothing you could have done.

EMMA. 'cuz I'm just a little girl, right?

I WAS SURE TO THE CORE
I WAS MORE, BUT I JUST DIDN'T SEE
I WAS ONLY EMMA
PLAIN, BORING EMMA… JUST ME.

I thought, if I could just find something to be… something that could excite people, then I'd have a real adventure…

MUSIC NO. 24:
"REAL ADVENTURE"

MOM. A real adventure? That's what you want? A real
adventure?

HERE'S THE REAL ADVENTURE
TAKE A LOOK AND SEE
SPEND SOME TIME DISCOVERING
WHO YOU ARE, NOT WHO YOU SHOULD BE

HERE'S THE REAL ADVENTURE
WHO KNOWS WHAT YOU'LL FIND
ONCE YOU FIN'LLY FREE YOURSELF
FROM THIS STUFF YOU'RE HIDING BEHIND

HOLD ON TO YOUR DREAMS
THOSE FANCIFUL SCHEMES
BUT DON'T SHUT US OUT WHEN YOU DO
AND SHOW US WITH PRIDE
THE VIKING INSIDE
BUT SHOW US WHO EMMA IS, TOO

HERE'S THE REAL ADVENTURE
TAKE IT, DON'T MISS OUT
THOUGH YOU'RE SCARED OF FACING IT
THAT'S WHAT GROWING UP'S ALL ABOUT

I KNOW THAT IT'S HARD
BUT LET DOWN YOUR GUARD
'CUZ BEING A KID'S NOT A CRIME
ADVENTURE'S NOT FAR
IT'S RIGHT WHERE YOU ARE
IN FACT, IT WAS HERE ALL THE TIME
IT WAS HERE ALL THE TIME

HERE'S THE REAL ADVENTURE
WITH YOUR FRIENDS, YOUR SCHOOL, YOUR DAD
HAVE IT WHILE YOU'RE LIVING
LIKE I DO WITH YOU
YOU'RE MY ADVENTURE
THE BEST ONE I EVER HAD

(**EMMA** *hugs* **MOM** *very tightly.*)

MUSIC NO. 25:
"REAL ADVENTURE PLAY-OFF"

(**EMMA** *hands* **MOM** *all of her "Viking Gear" and the lights shift to…*)

SCENE ELEVEN –
INT. MRS. MUKHERJEE'S CLASSROOM

(The next day, right before Morning Announcements. **EMMA** *steps in the room, and all eyes fall on her; for the first time, she is dressed like a little girl. The class watches in awe as* **EMMA** *takes her seat.)*

MRS. MUKHERJEE. Well…perhaps I should start by congratulating Nikki Tibbles on winning the class vote for best World Discovery Day report. You can pick up your pizza coupon on a break.

*(***MRS. MUKHERJEE*** reads from her clipboard.)*

In class news, Zinzi and Sebby Ferdinand-Muñoz would like to invite everyone to their viola recital this Wednesday at 7:30 p.m. in Swarthmore College's Lang Hall. Cookies and juice will be provided. And I have a reminder here that Emma Katz's birthday party is this Saturday at 2:00. It seems that the party is Viking-themed –

EMMA. NO…uh, it's not. It's just a party.

MRS. MUKHERJEE. Very well, then… You're all so quiet this morning.

ZINZI. Does it have to close? The library?

MRS. MUKHERJEE. Oh. Well…that's a good question, I guess. See, the town council doesn't think there's a need for it, so they've decided to use their money somewhere else.

GUNTHER. It doesn't seem fair.

MURPHY. Yeah. I mean, sure, I thought the library was kinda boring. But then…

SEBBY. Then Mr. Sigurd came into class.

PASHA. And he told us all those stories.

SIMON. Uh-huh.

MRS. MUKHERJEE. Well, the council feels that your computers at home have more resources than what our library has to offer. And the library…

MURPHY. The library has Mr. Sigurd. Isn't that worth something?

KIDS. (*Ad lib*) Yeah, Right. Isn't it?

MRS. MUKHERJEE. I agree with you. But there's nothing we can do.

EMMA. Keep on sailing. That's what Mr. Sigurd would say… Sorry. I just think that if all those great adventurers took a chance on something they believed in, why can't we?

MURPHY. Because we're not great adventurers.

EMMA. Maybe we are. Maybe we could be. Couldn't we try to raise the money somehow? Show the town that the library is worth saving?

PHYLLIS. We could have a bake sale!

MURPHY. We could sell hoagies!

MRS. MUKHERJEE. These are wonderful ideas, but I'm afraid they won't be enough to raise that kind of money. We'd have to do something so large and so stirring that –

EMMA. What about a Viking ship?

KIDS. (*Ad lib*) Oh, no. Not again.

EMMA. I mean it. This could make the library even more special than it is. We could put the ship near the library and people could pay to see it. They could pay to see a real-live Viking ship and hear real stories of world explorers from Mr Sigurd.

NIKKI. Yeah. That would be a great idea if the boat was real.

ZINZI. It is, Nikki.

NIKKI. No it's not, Zinzi.

ZINZI. My mom showed me the ad for it in *The Swarthmorean*. Emma was telling the truth all along.

NIKKI. Zinzi, SHUT UP!

MRS. MUKHERJEE. Nikki Tibbles! That's a strike. Two more and I'll take that pizza away. Emma, finish your thought…

EMMA. That was it, really...the Viking ship might do it. Guys, this isn't pretend anymore. I'm not some imaginary person with some crazy scheme. I just want to help Mr. Sigurd. Please. I'm asking you as your friend.

(A moment of tenuous silence. Then:)

ZINZI. The boat is a good idea.

SEBBY. Didn't you say you already wrote the guy who owns it?

EMMA. Yeah. Ivan Sindri. But he never wrote back. So, I guess —

SIMON. Well, what if we all wrote him?

MRS. MUKHERJEE. Yes... That might work.

*(She hands **EMMA** a stack of paper.)*

Emma, could you pass out this paper please? Quickly. If we're going to write letters to Mr. Sindri, we'll need to get started.

EMMA. *(Beaming)* Yes, Mrs. Mukherjee.

(The scene segues to...)

SCENE TWELVE: EXT. EMMA'S BACKYARD

(**OLLIE** *bounds onstage, loaded down with presents and balloons.* **MOM** *is running after him.*)

MUSIC NO. 26:
"THE BIRTHDAY PARTY"

OLLIE. I got da pwesents! I got da pwesents!

MOM. Oh, Ollie, sweetheart. Let me grab those, please.

OLLIE. And werwz da Boofday Wady?

MOM. Now, that is an excellent question.
(Yelling offstage:)
Birthday Lady! Oh, Birthday Lady!

EMMA. *(Entering)* Do we have to do this now?

MOM. Sweetie, I think we've waited long enough. If we don't start soon, your birthday's gonna be over.

EMMA. I just thought…it was stupid of me to think anybody would actually come.

(**OLLIE** *walks over to* **EMMA** *and tugs at her sleeve.*)

OLLIE. I came to yow pawty, Emma. I made you a pwesent.

(He presents her with a hand-drawn picture.)

Dat's you. And dat's me. And we'w on ow advenchow.

EMMA. Which one?

OLLIE. Dis one.

(**EMMA** *hugs him.* **MURPHY BEAN** *enters alone with a small present.*)

MOM. Em…

MURPHY. Hi. Did I miss the party?

EMMA. No, we were just…thanks for coming. You're the only one.

MURPHY. Well…not exactly.

MUSIC NO. 27:
"YO, VIKINGS!"

(One by one, the **KIDS** *enter the backyard, toting presents.)*

ZINZI. Happy Birthday, Emma.

ALL. Happy Birthday!

ZINZI. *(Demandingly)* Say it, Nikki.

NIKKI. *(Begrudgingly)* Happy Birthday, Emma.

> *(A rather burly man in a mover's uniform, played by the actor playing* **BOTHVAR***, enters.)*

MOVING MAN (BOTHVAR). Happy Birthday! Sorry to interrupt the party, but I gotta know where to drop this thing off.

MOM. I'm sorry. What thing?

MOVING MAN (BOTHVAR). You don't know? Mr. Sindri told me you would sign for it.

EMMA. Mr. Sindri? The "Sons of Valhalla Hall" Mr. Sindri?

MOVING MAN (BOTHVAR). Same one. You must be Erma.

EMMA. *(With a degree of wonder)* Emma.

MOVING MAN (BOTHVAR). Sure. Whatever. Look…he sent a note to you.

(Reads:)

Ms. Red: A true Viking can save the day by changing the world around her for the better, and that's what you've done. Here's to many more adventures for you and your town.

(To **EMMA***:)*

So, where do we put the ship?

MOM. It's happening, Emma! It's happening! Yes! YES!

(Catches herself:)

Sorry. Mrs. Mukherjee, can you call Mr. Sigurd?

MRS. MUKHERJEE. You got it.

*(***MRS. MUKHERJEE*** exits.)*

MOM. I'll call the local news.

EMMA. Like on TV?

MOM. Like on TV!

EMMA. All right, everybody. Let's try to save our library!

*(The **KIDS** cheer as **EMMA** stands on something – a picnic bench, a piece of lawn furniture, a box, whatever. The important thing is that we finally see her become a leader, truly embodying the spirit of "chieftain.")*

EMMA.
NOW THE VIKING WORLD IS GONE
AND A NEW DAY HAS TO DAWN
BUT THE VIKINGS DO LIVE ON
CAN YOU HEAR THEM CALL?

IF WE ALL CAN PLAY OUR PARTS
AS OUR OWN GREAT BATTLE STARTS
VIKING SPIRITS, VIKING HEARTS
WILL BE WITH US ALL

SO, HEAR THEM CALLING, CALLING…

YO-HO-OH! YO, VIKINGS!
YO-HO-OH! GATHER AND JOIN IN MY CLAN!
YO-HO-OH! NOW THE ADVENTURE'S BEGUN
SO, CAN WE FACE IT AS ONE?
I KNOW WE CAN!

*(The **KIDS** all burst into chatter, making plans.)*

AS THE WINDS BEGIN TO BLOW
LET YOUR INNER VIKING SHOW
LET YOUR FRIENDS AND NEIGHBORS KNOW
THAT WE'LL MAKE IT THROUGH

WHEN AT LAST PUSH COMES TO SHOVE
IF YOU FACE THE STORM ABOVE
AND YOU FIGHT FOR WHAT YOU LOVE
VIKINGS LIVE IN YOU
SO, COME AND JOIN ME. JOIN ME!
YO-HO-OH! YO, VIKINGS!

MOM. *(Overlapping unexpectedly)*
YO-O-OH! YO, VIKINGS!

EMMA & MOM.
YO-O-OH! TELL ME YOU'RE READY TO SHINE!
YO-O-OH! NOW THE ADVENTURE IS CLEAR
AND THE ADVENTURE IS HERE
IT'S YOURS AND MINE!

EMMA.

> AND YO-O-OH, NOW WE COME TOGETHER
> YO-O-OH, NOW WE CAN BEGIN
> YO-O-OH, NOW WE CAN FACE THE STORMY WEATHER
> IF WE ALL TAKE ON THE DRAGON WE CAN WIN!
>
> YO-O-OH! YO, VIKINGS!
> YO-O-OH! GATHER AND JOIN IN THE FRAY!

KIDS. *(Simultaneously with* **EMMA:** *)*

> OH! YO! YO, YO, VIKINGS! JOIN IN THE FRAY!

EMMA, KIDS & MOM.

> YO-O-OH! NOW THAT WE KNOW WHERE WE STAND
> THERE'S AN ADVENTURE AT HAND
> IT STARTS TODAY!

> *(The* **KIDS** *scatter and exit.* **OLLIE** *approaches* **EMMA,** *holding her "VIKING" attire.)*

OLLIE. I fink dis bewongs to you.

> *(***EMMA** *grabs* **OLLIE** *'s hand and runs off. The scene shifts to… EXT. LIBRARY. A* **NEWSWOMAN** *stands in front of a camera.)*

NEWSWOMAN. I am standing at 121 Park Avenue in Swarthmore, PA, outside of Swarthmore's Public Library, where a crowd has gathered to view the arrival of… get this… an authentic Viking longboat. I'm told that the 29-foot Icelandic ship will be coming right down this street in moments and placed directly on the library's front lawn. The boat was donated by the Sons of Valhalla Hall in Asgard at the request of a group of fifth graders from Swarthmore-Rutledge Elementary School…

> *(By this time* **EMMA** *has arrived back on the scene, wearing her Viking gear, and holding* **MOM** *'s hand.)*

…and this has to be one of them. Little girl, what's your name?

EMMA. Emma the…Emma Katz.

MOM. Emma Katz, *Viking Explorer.*

MRS. MUKHERJEE. *(Offstage)* Yo, Vikings! Straight ahead!

*(The **KIDS** enter wearing homemade Viking outfits, led by* **MRS. MUKHERJEE**, *who is dressed up, too.)*

We thought you'd need a crew… Ms. Chieftain.

*(***OLLIE*** drags **MR. SIGURD** onstage.)*

OLLIE. Kwik, Mistew Sigewd! Weew be wate!

SIGURD. For what? Emma…children. What is this?

EMMA. We did something for you.

SIGURD. I don't understand.

EMMA. Look.

(The ship appears.)

ALL.

OOH, OOH, OH!
OOH, OOHH, OH!
AAH, AHH, AHH!

MOVING MAN (BOTHVAR). All right, Bone-Threaders. Thar she blows!

(When the ship is "docked," the **KIDS** *all climb aboard.)*

MOM. Make a donation to see a real-live Viking ship and hear tales of the Norseman from our very own Sigurd Torvaldsson. Climb aboard and save the library!

SIGURD. Emma, I don't know what to say.

EMMA. We all pitched in. It might not work.

SIGURD. And what if it doesn't? The adventure is what matters!

YO-O-OH! YO, VIKINGS!
YO-O-OH! GATHER AND ANSWER THE CALL!

EMMA & SIGURD.

YO-O-OH! NOW THE ADVENTURE'S BEGUN
IF WE CAN FACE IT AS ONE
WE'LL HAVE IT ALL

(The **KIDS** *raise a flag on the ship that says "SAVE THE LIBRARY.")*

ALL. *(cont.)*

> AND YO-O-OH, NOW WE COME TOGETHER
> YO-O-OH, NOW WE CAN BEGIN
> YO-O-OH, NOW WE CAN FACE THE STORMY WEATHER
> IF WE ALL TAKE ON THE DRAGON WE CAN WIN!
>
> YO-O-OH! YO, VIKINGS!
> YO-O-OH! GATHER AND JOIN IN THE FRAY!
> YO-O-OH! NOW THAT WE KNOW WHERE WE STAND
> THERE'S AN ADVENTURE AT HAND
> IT STARTS TODAY!
>
> HERE'S THE REAL ADVENTURE
> NOW WE SOUND THE DRUM
> HERE'S THE CHANCE WE'VE WAITED FOR
> SO, LET'S GATHER AS ONE
> AND HAVE OUR ADVENTURE
> ADVENTURE, HERE WE COME!

(The **KIDS** *and* **MRS. MUKHERJEE** *look to* **EMMA***, who salutes* **MOM** *and* **BOTHVAR***, takes* **MR. SIGURD***'s hand and steps to the bow. The scene freezes in time, but the flag waves in the wind. Curtain.)*

MUSIC NO. 28:
"EXIT MUSIC"

APPENDIX A.

This script is written for 14 actors and can be expanded to a larger cast if needed. Ensemble Classmates, Townspeople and Vikings have been included in previous productions. If a cast smaller than 14 actors is desired, *Yo, Vikings!* can be performed with a group of 10 by removing the following roles:

PASHA
PHYLLIS
GUNTHER
SIMON

Additionally, the actor who plays BOTHVAR/MOVING MAN plays the NEWSMAN, and the following lines of dialogue are redistributed:

Script Page	Original Line	Given to
16	PHYLLIS: The Ferdinand-Muñoz twins do have a point, Emma	NIKKI
17	PASHA: World Discovery Day?	ZINZI
19	SIMON: Neal Armstrong!	No one (Cut it)
34	GUNTHER: Oh, man.	MURPHY
38	PHYLLIS: I've got Sir Francis Drake	No one (Cut it)
38	SIGURD: Did you know he was a pirate?	No one (Cut it)
59	PASHA, PHYLLIS: You'll never be a part of the class	SEBBY, ZINZI
59	GUNTHER, SIMON: Emma, you can't wear that to school	MURPHY

64	GUNTHER: It doesn't seem fair	SEBBY
64	PASHA: And he told us all those stories	ZINZI
64	SIMON: Uh-huh.	MURPHY
65	PHYLLIS: We could have a bake sale!	SEBBY
66	SIMON: Well, what if we all wrote him?	MURPHY

APPENDIX B.
PRONUNCIATION GUIDE

NAMES

BOTHVAR	BAHTH-vahr
GUNNHILD	GOON-hild
GYDA	GEE-duh
HELGA	HEL-guh
HUGIN	HYOO-gin
MJÖLVERK	MYOHL-verk
MUNIN	MYOO-nin
NIDHOGG	NEED-hawg
ODIN	OH-din
OLAF	OH-lahf
SIGURD	SIG-erd
THORKLE	THOR-kul

PLACES

Asgard	AZ-gahrd
Jotunheim	YO-tun-hame

… and incidentally, these East Pennslyvania folks pronounce the word "sure" almost indistinguishably from "shore."